DRUMBEAT

Tomas Black

First Published in Great Britain in 2021 by

TEARDROP MEDIA LTD

Copyright © 2021 Teardrop Media Ltd

ISBN: 978-1-9161756-2-4

To friends and family who supported my efforts.

Foreword

Drumbeat follows the exploits of Captain Benjamin Drummond, an officer in the British military and a cyber warfare specialist assigned to GCHQ. Drummond first appeared in my debut novel *The Omega Sanction*, which is a contemporary crime thriller set in the financial centres of London and New York. *Drumbeat* is set ten years earlier when Drummond was still a serving officer in Afghanistan, but, as you'll see, London and New York play a key role in the conflict as do the intelligence agencies of both countries.

While *Drumbeat* is the prequel to *The Omega Sanction*, reading one before the other will not affect your enjoyment of either story.

Insertion

1

Helmand Province, Afghanistan, 2010

Captain Benjamin Drummond woke from a troubled sleep to the sound of aircraft engines. He looked around, briefly disoriented by his surroundings, then remembered he was aboard an RAF Hercules somewhere over Helmand Province. The four huge turboprops of the C130 had been pounding his brain for the past two hours before sleep eventually took him. He sat alone inside the empty cargo hold with just his thoughts for company, bathed in the subdued red glow of a nightlight.

He shifted uncomfortably against the hard aluminium seat and tried to relieve the cramp in his stiff legs. He mentally went through the gear which had been methodically strapped to him on his brief stopover at Camp Bastion: a special ruggedised laptop and additional battery packs; a small folding communications array and a specially adapted frequency scanner, courtesy of GCHQ. Miraculously, his equipment had all made it in time from London. The lads at Bastion had laughed after they had finished kitting him out. "What about your weapon, Drum", one bright spark quipped. Trust the army to shorten a name, and over the years the name had stuck. "There ain't no room", said another. "We forgot his fucking parachute!" He'd settled for just his old Browning sidearm. It was a big, heavy gun unlike the more modern 9mm weapons his comrades carried, but it had the added advantage that when you ran out of ammo, you could always club the enemy over the head with it.

A hatch opened at the rear of the cargo hold, momentarily illuminating the cabin. An airman, dressed in the olive-greens of the

RAF, emerged from the main flight deck and made his way over. He wore the large green helmet and comms set of a loadmaster. Everyone called him Taffy. Drum looked at his watch. It was time.

"You're awake then," said Taffy, holding out a small flask. "Thought you could use some of this. Best coffee in Helmand." Drum gratefully accepted the flask. "Thanks. I have a pounding headache."

The airman reached inside his breast pocket and withdrew a small packet of tablets. "Here, take two of these. They'll help. It's the altitude. We're at eleven thousand metres and the captain has reduced cabin pressure in prep for your jump." He reached over and pulled a breathing mask attached to a small oxygen cylinder from a rack and handed it to Drum. "We must start you on oxygen soon before the jump—to flush out any nitrogen from your blood." Taffy pulled another cylinder from the rack and attached it to his belt. He hung the mask around his neck.

Drum put the mask to his face and turned on the flow of oxygen. He breathed deeply and immediately felt better. He continued breathing for a few more minutes, then placed the cylinder on the seat beside him. He poured himself a coffee and popped the two pills. The coffee was lukewarm but the best he'd ever tasted—at least at eleven thousand metres.

"Blimey, Drum, you must have royally pissed off someone to get us lumbered with this mission. What did you do—screw the general's daughter?"

"Sorry about that, Taffy. It came as a surprise to me too."

"Yeah, well, the skipper wasn't too pleased either. We were scheduled for the last flight back to Blighty. End of our tour. 'What the fuck has Ben Drummond got us into this time', he says. 'Fuck knows', I say, 'but it must be bad if they're dragging the poor bugger back from London to this shit hole'."

Drum smiled grimly. He'd barely had time to see his father before they had come for him. He's needed back at GCHQ urgently, they'd said.

"But you've only just stepped through the door!", his father had protested. "There must be someone else."

That's what he'd said. But McKay had insisted. He'd worked with the man in Iraq and later in Helmand. Major Angus McKay of Military Intelligence—now there's a contradiction in terms.

Taffy turned his attention to his comms and tapped the side of his headset. "Roger that." He turned to Drum. "We're twenty minutes to target. Better get you ready."

Drum stood and adjusted his webbing. The plane banked slightly, and he steadied himself against the fuselage. Taffy moved over to a locker and removed Drum's chute from its storage area. He helped him strap it on, carefully checking each clip and adjusting the harness. It was a tight fit with all the other gear strapped to him.

"Blimey, Drummond. A HALO jump is hard at the best of times. But with all this gear ..."

"You trying to cheer me up?"

"Sorry, just saying that you must be mad." Taffy looked at his watch. "Four-thirty. It'll be coming up for dawn over Helmand, but your descent should still be concealed."

"Thanks."

Taffy pulled another oxygen cylinder from its rack and a full facemask. "Time to breathe ox."

Drum took the cylinder and clipped it to his belt and pulled the mask in place. He breathed deeply, letting the oxygen flood into his bloodstream. Taffy held up his two hands—ten minutes.

Drum moved back towards the rear cargo door and steadied himself against the plane's bulkhead. Taffy followed, handing Drum his helmet and goggles. Drum pulled them on and then reached inside a pocket and found his gloves. The air outside was somewhere around minus forty-five degrees centigrade, cold enough to give him frostbite.

There was a dull hiss from around the cargo door as the cabin pressure equalised with the freezing outside air. A red light flashed overhead and the plane's rear fuselage cranked itself open, revealing the first breaking rays of an Afghan dawn. Drum was hit by an icy blast.

The plane suddenly lurched into a steep bank. Drum grabbed a loose piece of cargo webbing with one hand and Taffy with the other. The crewman came close to being flung from the hold.

The plane levelled out and Drum released his grip on Taffy's arm. The airman scrabbled for the safety of the bulkhead webbing and held on for dear life. The sky brightened from the light of a dozen red flares being ejected from the sides of the plane—aerial countermeasures against heat-seeking missiles.

Taffy pressed his hand against the side of his helmet, listening to his comms. He tore his oxygen mask from his face. "We're being radar-painted by a SAM", he shouted over the howling wind ripping through the cargo hold.

The plane banked into a steep roll. More flares spun out from beneath it, creating a white smoky trail behind them. No good against a radar-guided missile, thought Drum.

Taffy listened intently to his headset. He looked at Drum, kitted out and ready to go. He smiled weakly. "Time to fuck off, Captain Drummond." He let go of the webbing and pushed Drum out of the plane.

2

Sergeant Ian (Brock) Ives sat cross-legged atop the bonnet of his Land Rover, smoking the remains of his tobacco in a long, thin roll-up. He'd long ago run out of his regular smokes. Flecks of grey sandy desert clung to his three-day growth of beard, making him look prematurely old.

It had been a long night, and the men were exhausted. They had spent hours searching the cold, barren desert for their man.

Their orders had come direct from Major Angus McKay. He had little time for so-called Military Intelligence. Leave cancelled, they said. You're being redeployed. So here he was. Stuck in some nameless desert in the middle of Helmand Province, surrounded by Taliban, trying to find their 'package'.

The man had performed a HALO jump, so desperate was London to get him here. Brock shuddered as he remembered his own experience of the manoeuvre. His had been a training exercise, jumping from the back of a Hercules from five thousand metres. He'd felt claustrophobic in the breathing mask; without it, he would have been unconscious in less than thirty seconds. And the cold. Like flying through a meat locker. That was the 'High Altitude' part over. Then the warm air hit you like a brick, and you gritted your teeth waiting for the chute to open at a little under one thousand metres or the 'Low Opening' part —you hoped.

Brock watched the cold Afghan sky pale and swore. If they sat here much longer he would become permanently welded to the cold metal of the Land Rover. With so little planning, none of them had thought to pack any warm gear. He shifted the M16 lying across his legs and tried to get more comfortable. Shit, if they stayed exposed on this flat open desert, the Taliban would have a field day.

He regarded what remained of his roll-up with disdain and scrutinised Dick (Poacher) Davis out of the corner of his eye. The lanky man was leaning against the side of the Land Rover, smoking a filtered Embassy.

"Hey, Poacher."

"Yes, Brock."

"Got any Embassy?"

"Yes, thanks."

"Fuck you, Davis."

"Charmed I'm sure!"

He glanced at the tall trooper taking long calculated drags on his cigarette, relaxed and without a care in the world. An ex-gamekeeper with a soft West Country accent, Poacher was used to playing the waiting game.

Brock returned his gaze to the sky. "It'll be light soon."

Poacher nodded. "We'll stick out on this plain like a boil on a whore's arse all right."

Brock flicked away the remnants of his cigarette and slowly unwound his legs from beneath him, easing himself down from the bonnet, stretching and rubbing his hands to get warm. He turned to find Joe Cairns, the driver for this mission, still asleep, head back, mouth open and snoring loudly. What a racket. If the insurgents don't see us, they'll fucking well hear us. Brock had not known Cairns long. The rest of the troop had named him 'Charming' owing to his complete lack of social graces. What luck being stuck with the guy for six hours solid!

In the other Land Rover, Major Tim Weekes was arguing the toss with Tommy McPherson and Anil Prakash on what to do next. McPherson—known as 'Hazard' on account of the scary things he did with explosives—was pointing animatedly at the map; Anil Prakash, a tough little soldier, originally from the Gurka regiment, was shaking his head. Whatever Weekes was selling, they weren't buying.

Brock mentally went through the game plan. Get the man in, Weekes had told them. He recalled the Major's gaunt features illuminated in the harsh light of the projector in the cramped mess room of Station One just a few days ago.

"The enemy has something interesting," Weekes said, "and we need to know about it—or at least London does." He tapped a fresh cigarette on top of the projector and used it as an impromptu pointer, running a hand through his lank blond hair. "It was spotted during the last recce and photographed. We don't think its radar—probably communications. London's sending a specialist."

What a blinder of an idea, thought Brock. The insurgents are kicking our arse in Helmand and London wants to send a 'specialist' for a peek at a satellite dish. A few more Tornadoes would be more like it. Poacher had the right idea.

"Why not pound it from the hillside?" asked Poacher, stretching out his long legs, trying to get comfortable on the hard mess chairs.

A match was struck from the corner of the mess, its light revealing the thick-set features of McKay hewn from the shadows. The white smoke of a cigarette rolled over the flame and extinguished it. "It's information that wins wars, don't let's forget that. We need to know what information this technology is sending—or receiving."

The room remained silent.

Weekes contemplated the end of his cigarette. He rolled it between finger and thumb, then tapped it once more on the projector. "As I was saying, London is sending a specialist. A chap from GCHQ. His name is Captain Benjamin Drummond. He'll be the package."

The entire operation had been McKay's idea.

Getting the man in would not be the problem; getting the man out … not even Weekes believed that.

3

Drum tumbled head over heels as he fell from the plane, the icy air buffeting him every which way as it raced up to meet him from the desert below. Remember your training, he told himself, and spread out his arms and legs to bring himself back under control.

Taffy had pushed him out of the plane too early, which meant he would miss the LZ. He tucked himself into a ball, encumbered by the weight of the gear strapped to his front, and flipped himself onto his back. He watched the plane recede into the distance, then realised it was being chased by a white contrail that was closing fast from behind. There was a sudden flash of light, followed by a massive explosion which enveloped the plane in a fiery ball, breaking it into a thousand shards.

The concussive force from the blast smashed into his body, sending him into an uncontrolled spin. His vision dimmed momentarily, and unconsciousness threatened to take him. The voice of his old drill sergeant rattled around inside his head: *don't just lie there, Drummond, move yourself.* He painfully stretched out his arms and legs and spread-eagled once more. Then it hit him. A wave of warm air from the desert below.

Shit, he'd left it too late.

He glanced at the altimeter strapped to his arm. It read twelve hundred metres. The ground was coming up fast. With an effort, he tumbled forward into a dive, craning his neck just as the sun broke over the mountains in the east, their snow-capped peaks ablaze in a fiery orange glow.

It was now or never. *Move, move, you lazy little man.*

He pulled his ripcord and said a silent thanks to Taffy as his chute unfurled then fully inflated, yanking his harness tight with a bone-shaking jolt. He was still coming in too hot. He reached for the control handles of his chute with frozen hands. With an effort, he pulled both down together and his glide-plane flattened out, slowing his descent as he gained more forward momentum.

He started searching for a place to land. The terrain was typical of the coarse desert areas found in Helmand Province: grey rock and sun-baked sand, frozen to near zero at night under cloudless Afghan skies.

Dawn was paling to morning, and he risked being spotted by one of the local tribes. There was a bounty on all British soldiers and he knew the Taliban would take great delight in interrogating him. He circled and spotted a shallow ravine on his right. That might be useful. To his left was rocky, open ground. Less cover. In the distance, the ground grew more barren and merged into the foothills of a small mountain range. It was time to decide.

Drum circled down in the cool morning air and headed for the edge of the ravine. Here and there, rocky outcrops jutted up like broken teeth. He pulled down hard on both handles and flared out his chute as the ground came up to meet him. With one last tug, he touched down on the sandy floor beside the ravine and, with a quick hop and a jump, brought himself to a complete stop.

The tan-coloured fabric of his chute blended well with the harsh desert landscape. He quickly reeled it in, then drew his knife and cut the cords before untangling himself from the harness. He knelt, exhausted, and said a silent prayer for Taffy and the rest of the crew.

The ravine proved to be more of a shallow gash in the landscape than any substantial formation that might afford him some cover. The only feature of note was a large rock formation that rose out of the sandy soil and supported a sparse assortment of withered shrubs. That would have to do. The ground beneath him was already warming with the rising sun. He forced himself to his feet and gathered up his kit.

Drum searched his gear for a small folding shovel and moved to the base of the rocky outcrop and started digging. The soil proved easy to remove, and he was careful to keep the bleached topsoil separate from the darker spoil beneath. It looked more like a shallow grave than a hide, but then beggars can't be choosers. The thought sent a chill down his spine. He pushed it aside and kept on digging. In the process he'd dislodged an assortment of scorpions, which he hoped wouldn't return to reclaim their space in the shade. At least he'd have company.

Sweat trickled down his back and soaked his shirt. After twenty minutes, he stopped and listened. The low whine of an engine drifted across the open plain: a Land Rover or a heavier vehicle, perhaps, still some way off. The chances of his troop finding him were slim to none: he'd landed too far from the original LZ and they had no way of knowing his position. His hide would have to do.

He retrieved his gear and placed it at the end of the depression, just under the base of the outcrop, and buried the remnants of his harness close to a withered bush. He used the chute to camouflage the entrance to his hide, sprinkling the dry topsoil on top to disguise his handiwork.

The engine noises grew louder and more distinct. Not the engine of a Land Rover, but a much bigger vehicle with a chunky diesel. A second engine now accompanied the first, which had the distinctive high-pitched whine of a track bike—a mode of transport favoured by the Taliban. He drew his weapon and slid beneath the chute.

Minutes passed, and he lay in his shallow grave barely breathing. The engine whine of the bike reached a crescendo before stopping close to the edge of the ravine with a scuffing of tyres against the gravel and sand. Its exhaust clattered loudly as the engine idled. The ground shuddered under the wheels of a much larger vehicle as it rumbled to a stop farther from the hide. The exhaust of the bike fell silent and he heard the dull thud of boots on the ground..

The sand shifted alarmingly around the entrance to the hide and for a moment Drum thought he had been discovered. He gripped his gun. A man shouted in what he thought was Pashto, one of the many dialects spoken in Afghanistan. Another pair of boots approached the hide with slow, purposeful strides. Sand trickled down around the edges of the chute and something scurried over his hand. There was silence and then the start of a conversation. He recognised a few words. They were speaking Russian.

The conversation continued for less than a minute. Drum held his breath, daring not to move, dust and sand stinging his eyes. Then the hide was once more filled with the noise and exhaust fumes of the bike. Its tyres bit into the gravel as it took off away from the ravine, its engine whine decreasing into the distance. There was a scuffle next to the entrance and Drum could just make out the toe cap of a tan-coloured boot. It remained there for a minute, then withdrew. He heard the casual footfall of someone slowly walking away.

Drum let out his breath and blinked grit from his eyes. He raised his gun and gingerly lifted the chute. A crack of light spilt into the hide and he peered out, squinting into the bright sunlight. A group of maybe six well-armed soldiers stood around what looked like a GAZ Tigr, Russia's answer to the American Humvee, decked out in desert tan. A big man had his back to him, his peaked cap pulled over a mop of blond hair. He appeared to be the one in charge. They looked like a tight crew, relaxed and smoking as their man outlined the game plan. Some things never change, thought Drum. There was a squawk from a radio. The operator leant out of the GAZ window and shouted a few words in Russian. The troop sprang into action, dropping their cigarettes as they clambered back into their vehicle. The big diesel fired up. There was a clunk as the driver slammed the Tigr into gear, spinning the tyres before taking off in a cloud of dust.

Drum waited as the noise from the engine faded to silence. He relaxed, a wave of fatigue running through him. He'd never felt so tired. The events of the night suddenly came home to him. The plane, Taffy—all gone. And for what? He had no idea what the Russians were doing here. There were too many questions.

Drum flinched as something crawled across his cheek. He brushed a hand across his face and realised he must have fallen asleep. *Move you lazy bastard, move.* He poked a crack in his camouflage and peered out onto a bright, desolate plain. He dragged himself out on his belly and sat with his back against the rocky outcrop, which was now hot from the midday sun. He reached for his kit and found his canteen. Water never tasted so good.

Drum laid out the rest of his gear and retrieved a small GPS device and the GCHQ transceiver. He logged his position and realised he'd missed the LZ by many kilometres. He noted the time. An X-Band satellite would soon be overhead and he couldn't afford to miss the slot. He took a small folding antenna, expanded it like an umbrella and set it atop the rocky outcrop. He plugged the trailing lead of the antenna into the transceiver and turned it on. The system gave a soft whine as he dialled in a preset frequency.

"Grey Wolf, Grey Wolf, this is Rabbit, over."

The radio remained silent. He checked the time, then adjusted the antenna. The satellite should be in range.

"Grey Wolf, Grey Wolf, this is Rabbit, over."

"Rabbit, this is Grey Wolf receiving Lima Charlie, over."

He breathed a sigh of relief.

"Roger, Grey Wolf. Be advised, LZ is compromised." He paused. "Big Bird is down. Repeat, Big Bird is down, over."

The radio fell silent for a few seconds. "Roger that. Will send in air support for extraction, over."

That was the last thing he wanted. "Negative, Grey Wolf, Negative. Airspace too hot. I'm sending you my coordinates."

Again the radio fell silent. In his mind he saw the Grey Wolf unit leader debating the move.

"Roger that, over."

He plugged his GPS unit into the transceiver and pressed SEND. Somewhere overhead a satellite would receive the transmission as a burst of encrypted radio in the X-Band frequency and forward his coordinates to his unit. Hopefully, they weren't too far away.

"Rabbit, this is Grey Wolf, received. Stay put."

"Roger that, and out."

Brock had drawn the short straw and rode next to Charming as their Land Rover bumped and rattled over the rocky ground. God, the guy had terrible BO. But he guessed they all had—no one had bathed in over a week. Stands to reason, he thought. We must all stink.

Poacher sat in back, one leg dangling over the side of the vehicle as he read off the coordinates from his hand-held GPS device; Hazard stood in the back, holding onto a mounted GPMG as he scanned the horizon.

"We must be close," said Poacher. "Head straight for that ravine. He's somewhere in there."

Charming grunted and floored the accelerator.

"Fuck me," complained Brock. "Take it easy. My arse is already black and blue."

Charming smiled and eased off the gas. "Right you are, Sarge."

They slowed as they approached the ravine and crunched to a halt within a few metres of a rocky outcrop. Hazard stood on tip-toe and peered over the top of his machine gun. He scanned the horizon once more. "You sure this is the spot?"

Poacher stretched and unwound his legs from inside the Land Rover. He jumped down, examining his GPS, scanning it from east to west.

"Yep. Right here."

Brock jumped down with his assault rifle and moved to the edge of the ravine. He saw nothing but sand and rock. If their man had been here, he wasn't here now. He noticed Poacher examining the ground. "Found something?"

Poacher bent down and picked up the remains of a long, slim cigarette butt. He smelt it. "Russian."

The rest of the troop raised their rifles and scanned left and right. Hazard racked back on the GPMG, half expecting the enemy to appear from some rocky cover. But all was silent except for the occasional whisper of a desert breeze. The troop relaxed.

"Perhaps he's done a bunk—or been captured," proffered Charming.

"He did say the LZ was compromised, said Hazard."

Brock thought he heard something. The shifting of fine sand, a scattering of gravel falling into the ravine. He was about to turn around when he felt the barrel of a gun pressed into his back.

"Captain Drummond, I presume?"

4

Major Angus McKay of British Army Intelligence scrutinised the screen of his laptop with increasing frustration.

"Fuck it. Get me a map, Sergeant." He threw the laptop onto his makeshift camp bed. He'd not left the operations room in days.

"Right, sir." Sergeant Harry Jones promptly marched out of the room.

McKay waited for the door to close, then straightened up and stretched, inflating his enormous barrel chest. He was a bear of a man that could fill any room with his presence. The bones in his back cracked back into place. He ran a hand over a face of ginger stubble. God, he was tired. He should take a break and grab a few hours' downtime. He'd not slept in days.

He went back through the game-plan in his head. It was straightforward. Get our man from GCHQ in. Perform the recce. Get him out. What had he not seen? He'd chosen the men himself. All experienced soldiers. He'd even argued for Drummond. The man was a pain in the arse, but the best tech they had. He'd not been too pleased with the recall notice. But orders were orders. Drummond knew that—most of the time.

Jones backed his way into the operations room with a rolled-up map in one hand and a large pot of fresh coffee in the other. "Detailed map of the Helmand area, sir. And I thought you could use some of this."

"Good man, Sergeant." McKay cleared a space on the trestle table in the centre of the room and laid out the map, pinning each corner to the tabletop with four large tacks. Jones found two clean mugs and poured them both some coffee. "Thank you, Sergeant. Now, where was the plane's last reported position?"

16

Jones scrutinised the map. "Here, sir. Just south of the Helmand and east of a place called Dishu. It's mainly desert."

"And where have our drones been disappearing?"

"Here … and here. All American made Predators, sir."

McKay studied the map. He absentmindedly sipped his coffee. "In the ballpark."

"Sir?"

Mackay placed his mug of coffee on the map and grabbed a pencil. He traced a fine line around the base of the mug, removing it to inspect his handiwork. "In this general area?"

Jones peered down at the coffee-stained map. "Yes, sir." He placed a nail-bitten finger on a feature at the centre of McKay's pencil ring. "You think this plateau is significant?"

McKay stepped back from the table and straightened up, once more eliciting a loud cracking noise from his back. "I do, Sergeant. One thing that military history teaches us is the strategic advantage of high ground. In this case, the elevation of this area would make it an excellent base of operations for any communications array and provide a suitable location for air defences."

"You think this comms array has something to do with our missing drones?"

"Maybe. That's what I hoped our chap from GCHQ would tell us."

"Captain Drummond?"

"Yes, I had to pull some strings to get him here. GCHQ was not pleased to send him back."

"Then we have to scrap the mission, sir. The plane's lost. All souls …"

McKay paced the room. "What was their last transmission, Sergeant?"

Jones moved over to his laptop and scrolled through a log of recorded communications from the RAF Hercules, each one labelled 'Top Secret'. "Zero four-thirty. Captain Miles reported that they were being painted by radar. He was attempting to manoeuvre when transmission ended. That was over four hours ago."

"Do we know their height?" asked McKay.

"As far as we know they maintained an operational height of eleven thousand metres—well out of range of anything the Taliban have. In fact, out of range of most SAMs?"

"But not the Russians."

"Sir?"

17

"Growlers, Sergeant. Russian Growlers."

"You mean the S400 surface-to-air missiles? That doesn't make much sense—if you don't mind me saying, sir."

"I don't mind, Sergeant. It doesn't make much sense to me either. But it's the only thing that could have taken down that plane at that height from the surface."

Jones stared once more at the map. "If that's true then this would be a serious escalation of the conflict. The geopolitical implications ..."

McKay turned to face his Sergeant. "But it's just speculation at this point, so let's not get our knickers in a twist."

"But sir, even if it were true, how would the Russians get those kinds of assets into Afghanistan without being detected?"

McKay studied the map. "There are only two possible routes. Pakistan to the South via one of the Taliban supply lines into the region, or ...", he traced a stubby finger across the map, "Iran to the west."

Jones looked up from the map. "Bloody hell."

McKay turned away from the table and picked up his coffee. "But without expert eyes on the ground, we're fucked."

"We still have Charlie One Niner on the ground, sir. Grey Wolf."

Yes, thought McKay. Major Tim Weekes. He didn't know what to make of the man. Not his first choice. But he'd volunteered. Typical public school type. A Cambridge man. He had more faith in the troop's Sergeant. A Stepney man. East London born and bred. Great in a firefight, but couldn't spot a communications array if it hit him on the head. They were out of options. The mission was a scrub.

There was a sharp knock on the door. It opened and a young corporal stepped through into the room and handed Jones a slip of paper. "Flash comms from Grey Wolf, sir." He saluted and left the room.

Jones scanned the communication, a smile spreading across his face.

McKay put down his coffee. "What is it?"

"It's Drummond, sir. He made it."

Intelligence

5

Geoffrey Rayner exited his taxi outside a smart Edwardian terrace in Mayfair. It was a rare treat for him to leave the sterile confines of his office in GCHQ and travel to London. The location of the Section 6 meeting was not a surprise to him. People in his line of work simply referred to it as 'the club'. By day the club was a respectable meeting place for well-heeled bankers and those cabinet ministers wanting to escape the Commons for a few hours or entertain in private; by night, things got a bit more interesting when the club played host to those members with more carnal pursuits in mind. It was one reason GCHQ had the place bugged to the rafters.

Rayner strode up to the main entrance and tugged on an ornate brass pull. Somewhere on the other side of the door, a bell jangled loudly. A young man in a red livery coat and starched white shirt opened the door. If there was one thing the Brits were a stickler for it was tradition.

"Morning, sir."

"Morning, Harper."

Rayner walked through to the lobby. It was very much an Edwardian affair, with ornately carved walnut panelling polished to a warm rich brown. It smelt pleasantly of beeswax. A large walnut desk stood off to one side and acted as the doorman's station. Behind the desk was a large array of pigeon holes where members received their mail. The lobby opened out into a larger reception area, lit by natural sunlight from a large vaulted skylight, which gave the walnut panelling a somnolent amber glow. Members usually conducted their business on the ground floor of the club which was comprised of a large library and a dining area. A wide sweeping staircase led to the upper levels where most of the extracurricular activities took place. A member and his mistress was an unending source of intelligence.

Rayner turned to the young attendant. "Where are our guests?"

"They're waiting in the library, sir."

"Good man. Have the kitchen send up some tea. Better include a pot of coffee for our American friend."

"Yes, sir. And sir ..."

"What is it?"

"We have an addition."

"Addition?"

"Yes, sir. A Major McKay."

"You mean he flew in from Helmand?"

"Yes, sir. Early this morning. Still in uniform. Dust still fresh on his boots ..."

"I get the idea," said Rayner. "Better have the kitchen send up some sandwiches."

"Right away, sir. Shall I announce you, sir?"

"That won't be necessary, Harper." He walked across the lobby and headed for the library. Tradition, he thought, can be a real pain in the arse sometimes.

He entered the library to the hubbub of voices. The Section chiefs never missed an opportunity to exchange gossip. Simon Rogers of MI6, a tall Yorkshireman in a dapper suit, was deep in conversation with the Treasury mandarin, Sir Rupert Mayhew. Officially, Mayhew was in charge of banking regulation; unofficially, he was the Section's bag man, skimming off untold millions from various departmental budgets to fund the Section's black ops, thus allowing the Cabinet Office complete deniability.

Across the room stood Major McKay looking out of place in his military uniform which was a little worse for wear after his long journey from Afghanistan. He was with Jack Marchetti, a tough little American from Brooklyn who represented the CIA interests in London. Jack was looking a little upset with the Major.

Mayhew's hawk-like gaze fell on Rayner.

"Ah, Rayner. Made it at last."

"Gentlemen, sorry to have kept you waiting," said Rayner, walking over to his favourite Chesterfield armchair by the window. The chair's aged brown leather enveloped him as he sat down, releasing a small sigh of relief as if greeting an old friend. He liked this chair. It was strategically placed with its back to the window, allowing him to look into the well-lit room while his fellow occupants squinted into the sunlight. It was an old interrogator's trick he'd picked up at MI5. Some habits were hard to break.

Rayner caught Marchetti smiling. He was no stranger to interrogation and recognised the tactic. He was the first to speak, his demeanour suddenly turning sour.

"The Major, here, has some disturbing news. If his theory is correct, it represents a serious escalation of the current conflict in Afghanistan."

Rayner regarded McKay, who seemed unfazed by the American's assessment. "All in good time, Jack. Let's all take our seats. I've ordered up some tea and sandwiches from the kitchen. The Major here has had a long journey from Helmand and is probably in need of some refreshment."

"You Brits and your damned tea …" retorted Marchetti.

As if on cue, there was a rattle of crockery as one of the club's waiters wheeled a trolley into the library.

"Thank you," said Rayner. "Close the doors on your way out and no-one is to enter, understood?"

"Yes, sir," replied the waiter. He made minor adjustments to the plates on the tea trolley before exiting the library's twin doors and closing them with a solid thud.

Rayner reached over and picked up a small remote from a table beside his chair and pressed a red button. There was a loud clunk from the library's doors as concealed bolts slid into place, locking them in. The two full-height windows turned a milky translucent white and a large projector screen moved slowly down from a concealed area in the ceiling to cover the front of the ornate fireplace. Rayner pressed another button and a detailed map of Helmand Province appeared on the screen.

Marchetti shook his head as he moved to the trolley and found his pot of coffee. "You Brits and your toys."

Rayner smiled. "Right, Major. Over to you. I understand you have new intel on the operation."

"Thank you, sir," said McKay. He moved to a table in front of the fireplace and retrieved a similar-looking remote. He pressed a button and a diagram overlaid the map.

"The circle in red," continued McKay, "represents the hot-zone—"

"The area in which our drones went down?" interjected Rogers. He moved over to the tea trolley. "Tea Major?"

"Thank you, sir. Er, yes."

"Four million dollars," added Mayhew. "Three point two million pounds. The cost to the Treasury of each drone lost."

"Quite so," said Rayner, sensing they might be here until lunchtime. "Continue Major."

"Analysts at GCHQ suspect a jamming technology is in operation somewhere in this area." McKay turned on a laser pointer. He circled an area of terrain that featured a small plateau.

"Unproven," said Marchetti, standing next to the trolley sipping his coffee. "All you have to go on are a few blurry images of a comms array."

"Which is why the Major here put together this operation," added Rayner. "To prove or disprove the theory."

"And you now have boots on the ground?" asked Marchetti, returning to his seat.

"Yes," said McKay. "We dispatched a unit of our special forces out of Station One in Helmand to rendezvous with an asset from C Section —"

"C Section?" said Rogers.

"A new section formed from personnel drawn from the army's SIGINT and specialists from GCHQ," explained Rayner. "In effect, a new cyber-warfare unit. Still on the drawing board, which is why you haven't heard of it yet through official channels."

"Finally," added Marchetti. "The Brits make it to the twenty-first century."

McKay battled on through his presentation. "At zero four-thirty hours, the plane carrying our asset was lost on approach to the rendezvous." He circled an area just inside the hot-zone. "The last communication from the pilot reported they were being radar painted. The operational height of the transport was eleven thousand metres, thirty-five thousand feet."

McKay paused. The room remained silent as minds digested the information. Finally, Rayner spoke.

"And our asset?"

"He made it down, sir. The only survivor."

Marchetti shifted uncomfortably in his seat. "And your man claims it was a SAM?"

"Yes," said McKay.

"And you think it was a 'Growler' as you call them?" continued Marchetti.

"I do," said McKay. "The only thing that could have tracked and brought down that plane at that operational height."

"Growler?" said Mayhew.

"A Russian made surface-to-air missile—the S400. Very sophisticated," Rayner explained. "But what would the Russians be doing in Afghanistan?"

"The Russians aren't fussy who they sell their technology to," said Marchetti. "But I admit it's a worrying development. If the Major's assumptions are right, it could be the start of a new Cold War—or at least a proxy war, with the Taliban as the foot-soldiers."

"I thought the Taliban hated the Russians?" said Mayhew.

McKay put down his remote and moved over to retrieve his cup of tea. "The enemy of my enemy is my friend," he said, half to himself.

Rayner rose from his armchair and walked over to the tea trolley. They needed more intel. He poured himself some tea and turned to Marchetti.

"Jack, have the CIA any intel they can share with us?"

"No, none."

There was silence in the room.

"No, seriously, guys. The London station has nothing. Zilch."

Rayner turned to Rogers. "Simon?"

Simon Rogers said nothing. He turned his cup around on its saucer.

Rayner pressed him. "Simon?"

"We do have an operation in progress. A Russian asset is in play …"

"Simon, we need to know what our chaps on the ground are getting themselves into. If you can share any intel with us …"

"The operation—it's a work in progress. Picked up some gossip from one of our informants inside the Russian Trade Ministry. Boasting of a big arms deal going down. Not a top priority in the scheme of things. But …"

"Given what we've just heard," said Marchetti, "the intel could be significant."

"Right, right," said Rogers. "We would need to accelerate the operation. Oil the wheels somewhat."

"How much would you need?" sighed Mayhew.

"Probably a couple of million," said Rogers.

"Roubles?" asked Mayhew.

"Dollars," replied Rogers.

"That's a lot of lubrication," added Marchetti. "Can we do it?"

Rogers looked troubled. "We'll end up burning our agent in Moscow. She'll be finished."

No one spoke. They all knew the risks agents took in the service of their country. All that is except Mayhew, who risked nothing except red ink on his Treasury ledger.

"Right then," said Rayner. "That's settled. We carry on as planned and advise our chaps on the ground there may be Russian hostiles in the area. In the meantime, we'll activate our asset in Moscow."

"I'll get word to our operative," said Rogers. "She won't be happy. It'll be the end of her career in Moscow."

"Will she do it?" asked Marchetti.

Rogers turned to the American, red-faced. "Of course she'll bloody do it. She's British!"

6

Alicia Hartwood emerged from room 101 of the Moscow hotel and gently closed the door behind her. She casually looked up and down the corridor before surreptitiously hanging the 'Do Not Disturb' sign on the door and smoothing down her dress. She walked briskly to the elevator bank, her bright red heels muffled by the hotel's richly woven carpet. She pressed the elevator button to take her to the lobby and waited.

Alicia Hartwood was not her real name. She'd had many aliases over the years, but Alicia Hartwood of the British Trade Delegation in Moscow was one of her most trusted legends—at least she thought so. Tonight's debacle had changed all that. She steadied herself and forced her breathing to a slower rhythm. Stay calm.

A harsh chime announced the elevator's arrival. She looked around, but the corridor was empty. She stepped in and selected the lobby, breathing a sigh of relief as the doors shut tight with a thump behind her. She turned and inspected herself in the mirrored interior of the elevator car. She was no spring chicken, that was for sure. Well past her sell-by-date for this kind of work, but she could still pass for a much younger woman. Time had been kind to her.

She wore little makeup, yet her skin was fair and glowing, softening the crows-feet that were appearing around the corners of her pale-blue eyes. She reached up and adjusted her hair, which had started to turn a silvery-grey. She preferred not to dye it and smiled as she remembered her mother's opinion the matter: mutton dressed as lamb as she used to say. It would have hung long had she not bound it into a tight bun and secured it in place with an elaborate enamelled pin in the shape of a butterfly. A Swallowtail. A gift from a dear friend.

The elevator doors opened onto a large ornate lobby. It was nearly midnight, and the gilded patrons of the hotel were now tucked up in bed or otherwise preoccupied. She headed for the bar. She needed to report in and arrange an urgent exit from Moscow.

A lone figure sat at the bar. An elderly gentleman with steel-grey hair and a rod-straight back. A military man, like so many that frequented this fashionable hotel. His smart black overcoat glistened with the night's rain. He had not been waiting long. She saw him looking at her in the mirror that lined the back of the bar and nodded.

"Evening, Giles."

He neither looked at her nor smiled, but raised a hand to the attendant half asleep at the end of the bar.

"Evening, Alicia. The usual?"

"Better make it a double."

"That bad?"

"You could say that."

The barman, a young man in a starched white shirt, eventually appeared in front of them. Giles spoke to him in fluent Russian. He could well have been a Muscovite.

"Two gin and tonics. Make them large ones. And the good stuff. Not the watered-down horse piss you sell to the tourists, understand?"

The man straightened up. He probably thought he was dealing with one of the many GRU agents that frequented the place.

"Of course, sir."

Giles waited for the barman to move away before turning to face her. "What happened?"

Alicia thought back to the events of the evening.

"It started well—as we planned. Oleg was waiting in his room. I knew something was wrong as soon as I walked through the door. He was all smiles and smirks. A greasy little toad at the best of times."

"But he had the intel?"

"Oh yes. And much more …"

The barman returned with their drinks and placed them on two new white coasters. He nodded to Giles and made a swift departure back to his place at the end of the bar.

Giles waited until he was out of earshot. "More?" He took a swig of his drink. "I don't understand."

Alicia looked around the bar. It was still deserted, but time was not on her side. "Listen, Giles. I need to be extracted." She slipped her hand in his, discretely passing him a small memory stick. "Tonight."

Giles squeezed her hand and clasped hold of the device. Just two friends exchanging a moment of comfort. She withdrew her hand and picked up her drink.

"What happened up there, Alicia?"

"He knew who I was," she said.

"Not Alicia Hartwood of the British Trade Delegation?"

"No. My cover's blown." She took a large gulp of her drink. "Then things got interesting. Wanted more money … and a few other favours that don't bear thinking about."

"What did you tell him?"

"I told him to fuck off, of course."

"Was that wise?"

"Probably not. Then things got nasty."

"He pulled a gun on you?"

Alicia drained her glass. "No, it would have been easier if he had."

"Oh! I see."

"You know I'm no prude, and I always thought the guy was a little prick, but in his case, it turned out to be true."

Giles turned to face her. "What did you do?"

"I laughed, I'm afraid."

"Probably not a wise move with a guy like Oleg," said Giles.

"No," agreed Alicia. "He went berserk." She looked around the bar again and through to the lobby. Everything appeared as it should be. But things would not stay that way for long.

"Ok," said Giles. "I'll expedite the extraction order. You can stay with me tonight."

She took hold of his hand and gave it a squeeze. "Thank you, Giles."

"Where's Oleg now?" he asked.

"I left him in his room."

"I'll make sure London comes up with the additional money," said Giles. "Keep him quiet. He'll get over it."

"I very much doubt that," sighed Alicia.

7

"What do you mean she killed him!"

Simon Rogers stepped out from behind his desk in the MI6 offices and stood in front of the large window that overlooked the Thames at Vauxhall Bridge. He pressed his mobile phone hard against his ear, more in anger than anything to do with the quality of the signal.

Sir Rupert Mayhew looked up from his laptop, his finger poised over the spreadsheet of a ministerial budget which he thought could spare the several million needed to fund their Russian asset. He and Rogers had just spent the last hour working out the details.

"Problems?"

Rogers turned to regard the Treasury mandarin. "Hold on," he said into his phone. "I have Sir Rupert with me. I'm putting you on speaker. Just give us the skinny—no operational details." He returned to his desk, placed his mobile phone on a cradle and pressed speaker. "Our agent in Moscow."

"Good morning to you, Sir Rupert," said Giles.

Sir Rupert smiled. The calm voice at the other end of the line was obviously a seasoned MI6 agent. He could well have been any of the old Etonians that attended the club. "Do we have a problem?"

There was the slightest of pauses on the line. "Yes, sir. The asset in question demanded more money and … sexual favours in return for the intel. Our agent had no choice but to eliminate him. There was nothing else she could have done."

Rogers stood and banged the table. "I'll tell you what she should have done: got down on her knees and thought of England!"

The room fell silent. Sir Rupert raised an eyebrow over the rim of his small tortoiseshell glasses.

"I understand, sir," replied Giles. "And normally it wouldn't have been a problem. But our agent is an experienced professional and knew that his request was not typical of their previous encounters—he'd shown no interest in her before."

"So what are you saying?" said Rogers.

"Our asset was turned. He was acting as a double agent and this was his way of exerting his authority over her."

Rogers slumped back into his chair. He had to agree with this assessment. This was bad news. "And what of the intel?"

"I have reviewed it," said Giles. "I'm sending it via our encrypted satellite link. I believe the intel is still solid. It looks like our Afghanistan issue is a backroom deal by some creative members of the Politburo. I don't believe it's a fully sanctioned operation from their executive committee. But I'll leave the conclusions to our analysts."

"Where's our agent now?" asked Rogers.

"I put her on the first plane back to London. I'm afraid she's finished —at least in Moscow," said Giles.

"I'm certain of that," said Rogers. "The operation's over."

"Maybe not," said Sir Rupert.

"How so?"

Well, if this is just a few corrupt officials making money behind the backs of the Party's executive committee, there must be a 'bag man'—someone to launder their ill-gotten gains. Does the intel mention anyone like that?"

There was a pause on the line. "Yes," said Giles. "A name that comes up several times is one Dimitri Petrov."

"Ah, yes," said Sir Rupert. "Petrov."

"You know this man?" said Rogers.

"Not personally, you understand. It's my department's job to be on the lookout for large currency transfers—the proceeds of crime and all that. His name has come to our attention more than once. He's currently in New York doing battle with the Department of Justice who want to expel him and seize his assets. So far they've been unsuccessful in their attempts. He's a slippery character."

"How does this help us?" asked Giles.

Sir Rupert snapped the lid of his laptop down. "It's obvious. The bag man controls the operation. Through him, we find the buyers of the technology and those in the Kremlin who are doing the selling. We need to grab the bag man."

"How do you propose we do that?" asked Rogers.

"Well, not us," said Sir Rupert. "The Americans. There is someone who would love to nail Petrov. She's been trying for the past year. She works for the DOJ. We've crossed paths on several occasions. A real ball-breaker. Perhaps it's time for our friend Marchetti to meet with her."

"It's all we have," said Rogers. "What's her name."

"Delaney. Phyllis Delaney."

8

Phyllis Delaney stood on the steps of the Supreme Court in downtown Manhattan, her mood darkening like the sky above her. The courthouse was a large and forbidding building on Foley Square. Built in the Roman classical style, it was meant to convey the power of the law and strike trepidation into the hearts of criminals, but today's fiasco had made a mockery of that idea. She moved from behind a large granite column and pulled up her collar against the threatening rain. She realised her colleague and good friend Gerard Roderick was still talking.

"Sorry, Gerard, I'm miles away."

Gerard Roderick looked down at the diminutive figure beside him and stopped talking. He was a tall stick of a man in a dark, three-piece suit that contrasted with his dark-grey hair. He took two steps down to be level with her eye-line.

"I said it's no good scowling like that. We'll rally the troops and try another day. The evidence wasn't conclusive. All we had was a smoking gun, but no finger on the trigger."

Delaney sighed. "The evidence was crap. No wonder the jury couldn't decide a verdict."

"It was all our investigators could gather in the time," said Roderick, defensively. "We needed a break or a whistleblower to come forward."

"Our investigators had all the time they needed," said Delaney. "Their presentation was all over the place. Even I had a hard time following their logic. We have to do better than this."

There was a commotion outside the courthouse. The short, stocky figure of Dimitri Petrov appeared at the top of the steps, a black overcoat draped around his shoulders. He grinned at the sight of Delaney. Reporters raced up the steps to interview him.

"The conquering hero," mused Roderick.

"There is no justice as far as he is concerned," said Delaney. She turned up the collar of her raincoat against the threatening weather.

"Well, I guess he would argue differently. We presented a case—we lost. Justice was seen to be done," said Roderick. He smiled weakly into the scowling face of his friend. "At least that's the official line I'll tell the reporters as District Attorney."

The commotion grew louder as Petrov slowly descended the steps towards them, laughing and shrugging off awkward questions from the gaggle of reporters following in his wake.

"Hmm, I think he's coming over," said Roderick.

Delaney looked up and saw the grinning Russian heading in their direction. She turned and caught the eye of a large man standing beside a limousine at the base of the steps and beckoned to him.

"I see you've brought Earl with you," said Roderick. "Expecting trouble?"

"Just a precaution. Can I give you a lift uptown? I'm having dinner with Frederick Olivier. You should join us."

Roderick smiled. "Still hatching your plan?"

Delaney frowned. "We're serious about the new firm, Gerard. This latest debacle only highlights the need for a new type of investigative agency—one specialising in financial crime and corporate malfeasance. We would hire only the best investigators—specialists in forensic computing and accounting."

"The Pinkertons of the financial services sector," said Roderick with a smile.

"Precisely! Join us, Gerard. We'd make a great team."

"And what would we call this new firm?" asked Roderick.

Before Delaney could answer, Earl bounded up the steps and placed himself between her and the approaching Dimitri Petrov. At six-three and built like a tank, he towered over the Russian.

An ebullient Petrov threw up his hands in mock surrender. "Hey, I just want to talk. Let's keep this friendly," he said in heavily accented English.

"It's all right, Earl," said Delaney. "Let him through."

Earl stood to one side but stayed close to Delaney. Petrov took a cautious step closer.

"Better luck next time, Ms Delaney—Mr District Attorney. It was not your day." He grinned into the cameras thrust in his direction.

Delaney merely smiled, ignoring the jibe. She turned and started down the steps with Earl close by her side. She stopped and turned back to face Roderick, who was now fielding awkward questions about the case and why it had failed. "Think about it," she said, raising her voice to be heard above the squawking reporters. Roderick nodded.

She stopped when she reached the bottom of the steps and pulled out her mobile phone. She tapped out a quick message to Roderick: *We would call our new firm Roderick, Olivier and Delaney (ROD).*

"Is that her?"

Jack Marchetti rhythmically tapped the steering wheel of his prized Corvette to some nameless tune that had stuck in his head that morning. He stopped to glance at the petite woman in the beige trench coat walking down the steps of the courthouse towards a black limousine parked at the bottom. A large man followed her down, scanning left and right, occasionally turning to look behind him. A pro, thought Marchetti. He's keeping his principal close and constantly looking out for threats. He had good reason to be cautious. Dimitri Petrov had powerful friends—many ex-KGB—and would not take the investigation into his financial affairs lightly. There would be consequences. And Phyllis Delaney would know that.

He turned to the young woman sitting in the passenger seat beside him, a good looking Brit with a rope of copper-red hair. Petrov had a thing for red-heads. She would be their way in.

"Don't point, Harriet. It kind of gives the game away."

Harriet Seymour-Jones turned and flashed him a dazzling smile. "Sorry, Jack. I'm new to all this. And call me Harry."

Marchetti couldn't help but smile at her enthusiasm and her cut-glass British accent. He felt a twinge of guilt for what he was about to do. It wasn't something he felt often. Her involvement in the project had been Roger's idea. Marchetti had an inkling the man from Vauxhall Bridge was planning to recruit her anyway. He understood why. There was something about her. Not just her stunning looks or her gregarious personality; no, she had what the Americans called 'moxie': guts and determination. Nothing stood in her way. She'd get the job done. If she'd been an American citizen, he would have recruited her himself.

"Yes, that's her. Phyllis Delaney. The big guy with her, acting as her close protection detail, is Earl Johnson—war vet. Interesting history.

Did time for nearly killing a guy over a girl in Louisiana. Ended up on skid row. Delaney literally stumbled upon him on her way into the office. Some guy tries to mug her but hadn't reckoned on the little woman kicking him in the balls. The ruckus wakes up Earl, sleeping in a nearby doorway. He comes to the rescue, disarms the guy, and stuffs him into a nearby dumpster until the police turn up. Delaney hires him on the spot and the rest is history."

"Crumbs! Is that right?"

"Apparently."

They continued to observe the odd couple as they stopped at the base of the steps. Delaney was attending to her phone.

"She's younger than I thought she'd be," said Harry.

It was true, thought Marchetti. She looked to be in her mid-to-late forties, but her file said she was a good ten years older. It was hard to tell. She had a youthful, animated face, framed by a bob of platinum blond hair. Marchetti admired her. This unassuming woman held more power and influence than most of the CEOs on Wall Street.

"Our files put her in her mid-fifties," said Marchetti.

Harry wiped the mist from the windscreen to get a better look at their target. "No way!"

Marchetti turned to face her. "Look, Harry. I just want to make sure you know what you're getting yourself into. This won't be like one of those backroom accounting assignments you've worked on for the FBI. These guys can be ruthless—"

"I understand, Jack. Don't worry. I'm a big girl."

Marchetti frowned. "I think they made us."

"Really? How can you tell?"

"Years of experience, Harry. When they turn and point at you, it usually means the game's up. C'mon, let's introduce ourselves."

They got out of the car and walked over to Phyllis Delaney. Like a pro, Earl Johnson came forward to meet them. Marchetti, another pro, parted his leather jacket with thumb and forefinger on each lapel, showing him he was unarmed. Johnson turned his gaze to Seymour-Jones and determined that her threat level was low. He stood to one side and allowed them both to pass. It always amazed Marchetti the way big men underestimated the threat posed by a young, attractive woman. It was the first thing they had taught him in the CIA.

"Ms Delaney. Jack Marchetti. And my associate, Seymour-Jones."

Delaney glanced at her phone and smiled. She slipped it into her pocket and turned to Marchetti.

"I assume you must be from the FBI or the security services, Mr Marchetti. Although, your surveillance technique leaves a lot to be desired."

"You're not under surveillance, Ms Delaney," said Marchetti. He noticed Harry was smiling. "We were waiting for an opportunity to talk with you."

Delaney glanced at her watch. "Better make it quick. I have a dinner engagement uptown. What's this all about."

"We have a mutual desire to see a certain Russian behind bars. I believe what I have to say will interest you. Why don't we ride uptown together and I'll explain."

9

Drum sat beside the embers of a dying fire, trying to stay warm after a second cold night under a cloudless sky. He checked his equipment and reassured himself that all his gear was in working order. He had one last modification to perform on his GCHQ issued laptop before they broke camp. He had started to lay out a set of precision tools when the dulcet tones of the troop's sergeant interrupted him.

"You'd do better cleaning that old Browning of yours, Captain Drummond, than mess around with that pile of junk."

Drum smiled and set aside his precious toolkit. "Morning Brock. And call me Drum."

"Fair enough." Brock cast an eye over his equipment. "Hope this all this works."

Drum hoped so too. The price of getting him here had been a high one. He changed the subject.

"Why Brock?"

The sergeant run a hand though his dusty hair, revealing a silvery-white stripe down the centre of his naturally dark mop.

"Brock—like the badger. Don't ask me why it's there. Born with it." He shrugged. "Who knows?" He smiled. "Anyway, Poacher's got a brew going. Thought you might like one?"

"I'd love one," said Drum.

They walked over to a nearby Land Rover where Poacher was busy attending to a small stove. The scruffy-looking corporal called Cairns was asleep at the wheel.

"Morning, Brock, Captain," said Poacher, handing each man an enamelled cup of steaming brown liquid.

"Thanks," said Brock. "You're a lifesaver."

Drum gratefully accepted his tea and leant against the side of the vehicle. "Noisy bugger," he said, nodding in the direction of the snoring corporal.

"He can't understand why we call him 'Charming'," said Poacher.

"I 'eard that," said Cairns, opening one eye. He pushed himself upright in his seat. "Do I smell a brew?"

Drum smiled and handed him his mug. "Take this one."

"Cheers Cap."

"Call me Drum. Everyone else does."

"Thanks, mate," said Cairns. He took the mug in both hands, coughed up a large mouthful of phlegm and spat it onto the ground."

"Charming!" said Brock.

The corporal the troop had nicknamed Hazard walked up to greet them. "Morning, chaps. The Head-Shed would like the pleasure of your company this fine morning. New orders."

Brock gulped down his tea. "About time."

They found Weekes examining a digital map on his laptop which stood on the bonnet of a Land Rover. Anil Prakash, one of the few Gurkhas Drum had met in the SAS, was operating the secure radio. Drum assumed he'd recently downloaded the map via a secure satellite link. The troop had yet to think of a nom de plume for Prakash, but Cairns had taken to calling him 'Baby' on account of his smooth, hairless chin.

Weekes waited until the troop had all assembled, then removed a cigarette from a packet in his breast pocket. This was the cue for all the smokers to light up. Drum noticed Brock standing idly by as each soldier inhaled their cigarettes.

"Here," said Drum, handing Brock a fresh packet of Embassy. "I'm trying to give up."

Brock's face broke into a wide grin. "You're a star!"

"Gentlemen," said Weekes, using his unlit cigarette to point to the map. "New intel from London. It would appear that Captain Drummond's initial assessment of his contact was correct."

Drum wondered why the Major had been sceptical of his reported Russian encounter, but neither man had served together on any previous op, so he gave him the benefit of the doubt on this occasion.

"London believes there's a rogue Russian unit operating in the area —unsanctioned by the Russian government. Who they're working for is unknown at this point."

"You mean we're dealing with Merks?" said Brock.

"They seemed to be a tight unit," said Drum, "well organised and disciplined. More likely a Spetsnaz unit. Russia would disavow them if caught. We shouldn't underestimate them."

"Our orders," continued Weekes, "are to proceed to these co-ordinates." He pointed to a feature on the map. "Once there, we are to locate any ordnance that would pose a threat to NATO forces and retrieve intelligence from any communications equipment we find—that would be you, Captain."

"And what about the Merks, Major?" asked Poacher. "Do we take them out?"

Weekes frowned and hung the unlit cigarette on his lower lip. He pulled a battered lighter from his pocket and flipped the lid. He struck the wheel, lit the end of his cigarette and flipped the lighter shut, inhaling deeply.

"We are to proceed to target with the utmost care, avoiding contact with our Russian friends if possible. We fire only if fired upon." He removed his cigarette and flicked its end, scattering ash to the morning breeze. "Those are London's orders."

A murmur of discontent rang through the troop.

"No use getting our knickers in a twist," continued Weekes. "The politicians are trying to avoid an international incident. At least that's my assessment." He turned to Drum. "Captain. Have you anything to add?"

Drum was staring at the map. The feature that Weekes had pointed to appeared to be a small plateau. It made sense to place a communications centre at that point, but, without aerial reconnaissance from a drone, it would be difficult to locate. He moved closer to the map.

"Our previous reconnaissance showed our target to be in this general location." He circled the plateau with his finger. "But my guess is the equipment is mobile so it could be anywhere by now. It would make sense to keep it on higher ground—better for communications." He turned to Weekes. "I have the equipment to locate it—providing it transmits for long enough."

"And how do you suppose we make it do that?" asked Brock.

"We flush it out," said Drum. "Instead of driving straight to the target, we take a route that will allow me to monitor their comms traffic along the way. They must have a command-and-control centre somewhere issuing orders."

"What if their C&C is also mobile?" said Weekes.

"It's a possibility," admitted Drum. "But I'm guessing this is some sort of exercise—they're trying to prove their technology under field conditions. They'd want a permanent base of operations. Somewhere in the mountains."

Hazard asked the obvious question: "And what is this technology doing exactly?"

"GCHQ believes it could be part of a drone shield—a high-powered transmitter that swamps the aircraft's GPS signal, steering it off course. The Russians have been experimenting with the technology for a while. If it works, it would make our drones useless."

The troop fell silent as they digested the significance of this new information. Weekes snapped the men into action. "Right, we have our orders. Let's move out." He turned to Drum. "Which direction do you suggest, Captain?"

Drum pointed to the map. "This looks likes a good location. Due north east—a small hill with sufficient elevation."

"Sufficient elevation for what?" asked Weekes.

"A drone," said Drum. "We call in a drone."

10

Drum sat in the back of the lead Land Rover as it bumped and rattled its way across the harsh Helmand desert, en-route to their first checkpoint. He had rigged an aerial on top of a telescopic tent pole and was scanning for radio frequencies with his portable equipment. So far, he'd heard only static and the constant drone of Charming as he drove and chatted to Brock up-front.

"… and so I says to her: 'Kylie, I'm leaving on a dangerous mission. I may never see you again'—this was on Paddington station, you understand. So she looks at me kinda funny like and says—"

"Put a sock in it, for fuck's sake," said Brock.

"Yeah. How did you know?"

Drum heard the distinctive 'beep' from his equipment that told him it had located a radio frequency.

"Hold on, chaps. I've got a hit."

Charming slowed the Land Rover and gradually brought it to a halt. The other vehicle pulled up alongside. Drum read off the frequency and estimated a rough bearing. He would need two more readings from different locations to triangulate a fix of the transmission, but this was a start.

"Is it what we're looking for?" asked Weekes from the other vehicle.

Drum raised a hand to silence the Major as he attached a frequency analyser to his makeshift aerial and connected his laptop. He started the analysis of the signal.

"It's too early to tell," said Drum. "The signal is very weak, but it looks like comms traffic from a ground unit." He slowly turned the aerial, reading information graphically displayed on his laptop. "Not aircraft or drone communication." He tapped a few keys. "Not one of ours. More likely local icom traffic—commercial, off the shelf. They're in the ballpark."

Weekes turned to Poacher. "Davis, take the bike and scout ahead on Drummond's bearing."

Poacher nodded and climbed out of the Land Rover. He moved to the back of the vehicle and unbolted a track bike from its rack that each unit carried. He hefted it down and adjusted his gear, his long legs astride the bike. He rolled the bike forward until he was level with Drum and took the bearing.

"Don't get lost," said Drum.

Poacher smiled. "Wouldn't hear of it." He pressed the electric starter and the bike purred into life. "Back in two ticks …"

Drum watched as Poacher sped off, the back of the bike occasionally fish-tailing over the rocky ground. He tapped Charming on the shoulder. "Let's go."

Charming slammed the Land Rover into gear and headed in Poacher's direction. Brock checked the mag on his M16, then reached into his pack and attached an M203 grenade launcher. Brock always favoured the US-made carbine. The other vehicle followed behind with Hazard in the back, gripping the mounted GPMG, Prakash driving and Weekes riding shotgun with his regulation British issued SA80 assault rifle.

They drove on for another hour with Drum scanning the airwaves. They climbed in elevation, providing Drum with better reception. The signal was getting stronger with his analyser showing peaks in a non-military range of frequencies. There was definitely an unknown ground unit transmitting in the vicinity with radio chatter increasing.

The terrain became more rugged. Small, rocky outcrops punctured the grey desert soil. Here and there the gnarled trunk of a stunted camel thorn tree broke the monotony of the landscape.

Brock leaned out of his seat and studied the ground racing by. He tapped Charming on the shoulder.

"Slow down and pull over."

Charming eased off the accelerator and brought the vehicle to a stop. He raised his driving goggles.

"What's up?"

Brock jumped out of the Land Rover and squatted down, studying the hard, baked earth. He peered into the distance. Up ahead the ground rose on either side to form the beginnings of a shallow gully, the remnants of a dried-up riverbed. The second vehicle coasted to a stop a short distance behind. Brock raised his hand and balled it into a fist.

"Bike track. Not ours," said Brock. He turned and gestured to the other vehicle. "Back up nice and slow, mate. You too, Charming."

Charming screwed up his face. "Fuck it. We've driven onto an IED!" He put the Land Rover into reverse gear and slowly backed up as Brock jumped back in.

Drum turned his attention to his laptop and quickly scanned the radio spectrum. He was looking for any spurious frequencies, such as those used by mobile phones, that might trigger an Improvised Explosive Device. Phones were more likely near a town that needed a cellular tower to support them; out here in the wilds, it was probably something as simple as a length of wire or a pressure plate. Either way, the enemy was not far off.

"Nothing on the scope," said Drum. "Probably a wire or pressure trigger."

Hazard racked back on his GPMG in the vehicle behind. "Fuck it. Give me a target."

Drum barely heard it: the distinctive whine of a high-velocity round shot from a high-powered rifle. A few hundred metres ahead of them, a large shrub shattered, sending up a shower of broken twigs and leaves which danced and twisted in the hot desert air, before finally settling near a broken and bloody body.

"Poacher!" said Brock.

The tall figure of Poacher emerged from a small rocky outcrop to their left, holding his sniper's rifle—the British made L115A3. He walked casually towards them.

"Afternoon, chaps. You took your time."

Hazard jumped down from his vehicle. He walked over to Poacher and slapped him on the shoulder. "When did you spot him?"

Poacher shouldered his weapon and reached for his packet of Embassy. He shook out a cigarette and placed it between his lips.

"Noticed his bike tracks a few clicks back," explained Poacher. "I circled around and observed him from cover." He pointed to a large, woody shrub about twenty metres into the gully. "The IED is probably buried there."

Hazard sighed. "Give me a minute." He returned to his vehicle and pulled a shovel from the side and a small tool kit from his bag. "Better back up a little further."

The rest of the troop returned to their Land Rovers and reversed back the way they had come.

Weekes jumped out of his vehicle. "Take positions away from the vehicles and keep your eyes peeled for his friends—move it, chaps."

The troop dispersed and took covering positions on either side of the gully. Drum climbed to get some elevation and scanned the horizon for possible threats. He watched with admiration and some apprehension as the small stocky Scotsman calmly walked towards the explosive device. The rest of the troop looked on. If any were anxious, they didn't show it. They did their job and kept their comrade covered. The gully fell silent as Hazard bent and scraped away at the soil around the bush.

Drum let out a sigh of relief as Hazard finally stood, holding what appeared to be a brass shell casing. He carefully examined it, turning it slowly in his hands. Satisfied, he picked up his gear and sauntered back to the troop.

"Er, hold on to this," said Hazard, lobbing the shell casing at Charming. "Might come in handy."

"Fuck me, mate," shouted Charming, jumping up to catch the explosive in both hands.

"Don't worry mate, it's perfectly safe now," said Hazard smiling. "Nasty thing. A shaped charge—military-grade explosive. Not your average homemade rubbish. Made it slightly easier to defuse." He held up the detonator in his hand.

Drum stood and walked towards the dead insurgent.

"Let's get a look at our friend."

"Hang on," said Weekes. "Sergeant, go with him."

Brock grabbed his rifle and strode after Drum. "Hang on, mate. Our friend may have company."

Drum drew his ageing Browning and racked the slider. He waited for Brock to catch up. Brock grabbed him by the shoulder."

"I'll lead. You follow."

"Yes, boss."

Brock smiled. "The Major would never forgive me if I lost the package."

They made their way over rocky ground and up a slope of shale until they came to a large bush where they found their man. It was not a pretty sight. The high-velocity round had found its mark. Poacher, an expert marksman, had taken a headshot. At such close range, a headless corpse was all that remained.

"Jesus," said Brock.

44

Drum forced himself to examine the body. He was dressed as a local tribesman in a rough, cotton smock, a waistcoat and baggy tan trousers —typical of the Taliban insurgents in the area. Around his waist was a well-supplied ammo belt. Drum searched the man's pockets.

"Found it," said Brock, holding up what looked like an AK assault rifle.

"Found what?"

"An AK74 - an updated version of the AK47. Not something an insurgent would carry."

Drum pulled out a worn, flip-lid lighter from the soldier's waistcoat pocket. He handed it to Brock.

"The crest on the lighter," said Drum.

"Spetsnaz, or a gift from one of our Russian friends."

"Either way," said Drum, "they know we're coming."

11

It was just after sunrise and Drum lay prone atop the ridge, looking down onto the valley below. In the middle sat a small village. It looked peaceful. A few stray dogs meandered through a scattering of mud huts and an assortment of ramshackle concrete buildings. A patchwork of fields surrounded the dwellings. A trickle of a river, fed from the mountain range beyond, provided the only irrigation. In the distance, north of the village, the mountain range rose and topped out to form a small plateau. Drum passed his scope to Brock.

"There—in the centre—a large compound."

Brock put down his field glasses and placed the scope to his eye. "What am I looking for?"

"A large, white tarp providing cover for a vehicle just right of the central building."

Brock closed one eye and squinted through the scope. "Oh, yeah. I see it. Military vehicle. It's a GAZ all right. Looks like we found your Russians." He surveyed the rest of the compound. "Just one guard."

Drum peered through his field glasses. "No one else?" He looked at his watch. "Well, it is only 05:30."

"We should call it in," said Brock.

"Let's keep radio silence for now," said Drum. "They could well be monitoring our transmissions. Even though they're encrypted, it would signal our presence."

"Right then. We'd better get back to the rest of the troop before they send out a search party."

There was a scuffle of stones behind them. Brock instinctively turned, pulling his sidearm in one fluid movement."

"Fuck me. Where did they come from?"

Drum turned to find a small herd of goats. He laughed.

"Must be a new Taliban terror weapon—Stealth Goat."

Brock smiled. "Yeah, right."

A small head suddenly popped up from behind a goat at the back of the herd. Then a pair of arms and hands. The goats parted to reveal a small boy.

Brock aimed his weapon at the boy. "Fuck it! Now what do we do?"

Drum lifted his head and scanned along the ridge. "He looks to be alone."

"But he won't be for long once he gets back to the village and tips off his mates."

"Take it easy," said Drum, placing a hand over Brock's raised gun. "Lower your weapon. There's nothing we can do. He's just a boy."

Brock reluctantly lowered his weapon. "I've seen younger ones blow a man to pieces …"

The boy did not move. He stood his ground and stared at them.

"Well, he seems in no hurry to leave that's for sure," said Drum.

On a hunch, Drum beckoned him over.

The boy dropped to his hands and knees and crawled his way towards them. He sat back on his haunches and grinned broadly. He pointed to his chest.

"Hamid."

Drum pointed to his chest. "Drum." He pointed to Brock: "Brock."

The boy nodded. He pointed to Drum's scope.

"I think he plans to rob us," said Brock. "We should lob him over the side—just joking."

Drum handed the boy his scope—a precision instrument worth several hundred dollars on the black market.

Hamid put the scope to his eye and scanned the valley below. It seemed to Drum that he had done this before. He lowered the scope and pointed into the distance. Drum took back the scope and looked in the general direction the boy had pointed. There was a dust cloud on the road approaching the village.

Drum handed the scope to Brock. "Looks like our friend has spotted an approaching convoy."

Brock observed the road. "Cheeky little bugger."

The dust cloud in the distance was now visible with the unaided eye. There looked to be at least two vehicles. Just as the lead vehicle rounded a bend in the road, a large dust cloud enveloped the convoy forming a rising pillar of flame and smoke. A few seconds later the sound of an explosion echoed around the valley.

"Shit," said Brock, "that should wake everyone up."

Drum turned to Hamid, who was now smiling. The boy dropped to his hands and knees and edged back from the ridge. He paused and beckoned them to follow him.

"Time to leave," said Drum.

The two soldiers gathered up their gear and shuffled back, keeping low so as not to be seen. Once clear of the edge, they stood and started walking back to the area where they had hidden their bikes. Hamid raised a hand for them to stop. He pointed at his feet. He then turned and pointed to his left and raised his arms, miming an explosion. He turned to his right and did the same.

"Shit," said Brock, "they've mined the ridge with IEDs."

Hamid took Drum by the hand and started forward once more, ushering the goats ahead of him.

"Keep close behind me," said Drum.

"Like glue."

Drum noticed they were following the faintest of paths scratched in the dirt. The boy moved purposely, without faltering. After a few minutes, they had reached their bikes.

Drum loaded his gear. Hamid just stood and watched.

"He's waiting for something," said Brock.

Drum held out his hand to say thanks and goodbye, but to his surprise, the boy climbed up and over the crossbar. He looked back at Drum and tapped his chest.

"I think he wants to drive," said Brock.

"Or perhaps he wants a lift?"

"Either way, we can't spare the time. Chuck him off and let's get going. Weekes is probably going ape-shit."

Drum indicated with his thumb that the boy should leave. Hamid shook his head and pointed to Drum. He then tapped his chest several times.

"I think he wants us to go with him," said Drum.

"C'mon, Drum. Just chuck him off—"

"No, really, Brock. We should do as he says. I think he wants to lead us out of here."

Brock sighed. "Weekes will court marshal my arse. Let's move before we're discovered."

Drum hit the ignition switch on the bike and kicked it into gear. Hamid sat forward on the seat and reached for the handlebars. Drum sat behind him, his two arms reaching around the small boy. They took off slowly down the ridge in the direction they had come, with Hamid pointing the way. They travelled for about ten minutes until they reached a rough track strewn with rocky outcrops on either side and large boulders. The rest of the troop were camped further to the east. He brought the bike to a halt.

"I think you were right, Brock. We should call this in. The ridge may have shielded the rest of the troop from the sound of the explosion. We need to give them a heads up."

"What about giving away our position?" said Brock.

"I don't think we have much choice."

Drum reached for his radio but Hamid stayed his hand. He pointed to a large rocky outcrop ahead of them. Drum saw movement. A man, in traditional Afghan dress, emerged from the shadows. He appeared to be unarmed.

"Looks like we have company," said Brock.

The man took a few paces towards them, stopping short of the bikes. He stood smiling at the two soldiers. Drum noted his fine waistcoat over a smock of white linen. On his side, he wore the Afghan Choora, a long-bladed knife. Both handle and scabbard were richly decorated. His hair, like his beard, was jet black and well-groomed.

"I think this is the Head Shed," said Drum. Keep your hands where he can see them."

"Roger that," replied Brock.

The man looked at the boy and spoke a few words. Hamid beamed and climbed down from the bike. He ran over to the man and stood by his side. The man affectionally pulled Hamid toward him, cupping a large hand under the boy's chin. The boy looked up and spoke to the man. He pointed to Drum.

The man turned and raised his hand. It was a casual gesture, but the effect was immediate. More men emerged from behind the boulders and from the scattering of small trees and shrubs. Their tan and grey smocks provided them with perfect camouflage for the terrain. And, unlike their leader, each man carried an AK47.

12

Brock and Drum sat cross-legged on a fine Persian carpet which formed the centrepiece of a sizeable room in a mud-brick building which was part of a well-maintained compound. The man they called Asadi sat opposite, flanked by his two lieutenants. A small contingent of armed men stood a discrete distance from the main group with their backs to the wall, staring intently at the two Englishmen. Hamid sat close by, grinning. Drum couldn't help but notice the family resemblance between Asadi and the boy: the strong nose, broad mouth, jet-black eyes and hair. He assumed they were father and son.

Drum shifted uncomfortably on the hard floor. His legs were stiff from lying out in the cold all night observing their Russian friends. After summoning his men back at the ravine, Asadi's two lieutenants had climbed on the back of each bike and guided them to the compound. The soldiers had kept hold of their weapons. Drum reasoned they wanted to 'jaw, jaw, not war, war,' which was fortunate, as he estimated they were outnumbered ten-to-one.

"I wonder if we should have taken our boots off?" said Brock, looking down at the fine rug.

"Probably not a great idea," said Drum. "We haven't bathed in a week."

"Yeah, the stench from our feet could well cause an international incident."

Asadi noticed their conversation and spoke quietly to Hamid. The young boy jumped up from his father's side and ran to the door. He shouted to someone at the top of his lungs, and Asadi's men all laughed.

A young girl came into the room carrying a good-sized samovar and several small cups on a large pewter tray. Drum thought her to be fifteen or sixteen years of age—a woman in the eyes of the Afghans. She wore a brightly coloured purple dress over a pair of matching trousers that gathered around her ankles. On her head, she wore an emerald-green headscarf. Her eyes were the most beautiful Drum had ever seen: steel-grey, bright and wide.

The girl placed the heavy tray carefully in the centre of the rug and knelt down. She stole a glance in Drum's direction. Drum thought he and Brock must look a sorry sight. They were both cold, tired and hungry and neither man had shaved for several days.

Asadi spoke firmly, but not harshly to the girl and gestured in their direction. She responded in kind, lifting the lid of the samovar and giving the contents a quick stir. A waft of smoky tea infused with cardamon and cinnamon filled the room.

"Hope you like Kahwah," said Drum under his breath.

"I'm so parched I'd drink anything," replied Brock.

The girl smiled. It seemed to light up the room.

Asadi spoke again and gestured in their direction.

"Who is leader," asked the girl.

Drum returned the smile. So this was their translator. Brock tapped Drum on the knee, reminding him he was the senior officer.

"Captain Benjamin Drummond. British Army."

The girl quickly translated as she poured the tea. Asadi nodded and mouthed Drum's name.

"Thank you," said Drum, gratefully accepting a cup of the hot green tea. He took a sip and smiled, nodding appreciatively to Asadi. The man smiled back, and the tension in the room evaporated. Tea was passed to Asadi and his two lieutenants and a general hubbub filled the room.

Drum turned his attention to the girl. "What is your name?"

The girl reached forward and took his empty cup and refilled it. She handed it back and in a soft voice said, "My name cannot be mentioned in public, but I am known as Aisha. Abdul is my father." She nodded towards a lieutenant who was eyeing Drum with suspicion.

Drum chided himself for asking. The Afghan culture was not a liberal one and, as a British officer, he had to respect the local custom.

"Please tell your elders we are grateful to the young Hamid for leading us to safety, and Asadi for his generous hospitality."

She returned to the samovar and poured more tea for Asadi and his men, translating as she did so.

Hamid beamed and puffed out his small chest. Asadi nodded his appreciation to Drum for his kind words and hugged his son. He spoke quickly to Aisha.

"Asadi wishes to know why you are here."

Brock looked at Drum and raised an eyebrow. Their mission was secret, but they had clearly stumbled upon another conflict. Something more personal. He looked across the room at the men seated there. They looked battle-hardened and wary. Asadi was watching him closely, his dark eyes staring intently. Drum decided to give them some truth, but little detail.

"Our mission is to reach the mountain at the end of the valley and to observe the fighters there."

"Nice one," whispered Brock.

Aisha thought for a moment and translated. There was a stirring among the men. Asadi turned to his two lieutenants and an argument broke out.

"Or maybe not so nice," added Brock.

Asadi raised his hand and the conversation subsided. He spoke brusquely to Aisha. She shook her head and argued back. The one she called Abdul, her father, appeared to reprimand her. She lowered her head and nodded.

"I need to explain," she said, glancing behind her at the three elders. "Many men guard the mountain - Taliban and other foreign fighters. They came to our village from across the Pakistan border, many months ago. They took over the village, burnt down our school and killed many people. Then the Shuravi came and started building in the caves on the flat side of the mountain. They have turned it into a … great fort."

She glanced back towards Asadi who waved his hand for her to continue.

"Asadi, our leader, gathered what remained of our village and fled here. He gathers fighters loyal to him from surrounding villages, but the Shuravi are fearsome fighters." She paused and looked at Drum, her steel-grey eyes wide with anticipation.

"Asadi wishes to know if you fight the Shuravi?"

Drum was not familiar with the name and looked to Brock for inspiration.

"I think she means the Russians."

Drum turned to Aisha. "Russians?"

There was silence among the group. Asadi reached into his waistcoat pocket and pulled out a battered, steel lighter. He tossed it at Drum's feet.

Drum leaned forward and retrieved the lighter. Its flip lid was shiny from wear. He turned it over in his palm and noticed the emblem on the side: two oak clusters bisected by a dagger and the letter A. The crest of the Spetznas.

The room fell silent and Drum felt all eyes upon him. Asadi spoke softly to Aisha, but his eyes remained fixed on the two Englishmen.

"Asadi wishes to know your answer," she whispered.

Drum reached into his jacket pocket and pulled out a similar lighter. He tossed it at the feet of the men opposite. Asadi bent and picked it up, turning it slowly in his hand. He smiled and handed it to Abdul, whose face broke into a wide, toothy grin. He held his hand aloft, proudly displaying the lighter to his fellow fighters. Drum held up Asadi's lighter, and a great cheer filled the room.

"The enemy of my enemy is my friend," whispered Drum.

13

The troop had assembled inside the militia compound. Drum guessed that Weekes would not be happy with the new plan. For a SAS officer, he was a cautious man. They stood around the bonnet of one of the Land Rovers where Weekes had laid out a map. The rest of the troop were relaxing with tea, courtesy of Aisha and the women of the militia. Hamid stood on tip-toe, trying to see what was going on. He and Drum had become inseparable.

Weekes placed an unlit cigarette between his lips and scanned the map. He glanced down at Hamid, standing close to Drum. The boy looked up and smiled. Weekes frowned and returned his attention to the map.

"This is the Russian HQ?" said Weekes, pointing to a location on the map.

"Right, Major," responded Brock. "It's the largest compound in the village. The Russians are billeted there. We estimate a minimal force of about six to eight professional soldiers."

"But Spetsnaz," replied Weekes.

"Correct," said Drum. "The rest appear to be local Taliban fighters. Asadi estimates there to be around twenty men."

"And we don't know about the contingent of men inside the mountain base?" continued Weekes.

"Not for sure," said Brock, "although Asadi believes there may be a small group of Russians—not fighting men. Probably technical personnel."

Weekes tapped the end of his cigarette on the map, deep in thought. He then placed it once more between his lips and pulled out his battered lighter. He flipped open its lid and lit the end, taking a long drag.

"And you trust this man, Asadi?" said Weekes, eventually. He eyed Hamid who was smiling at the mention of his father's name but knew nothing more of the conversation.

"I do, sir," said Drum. "He's given us no reason to doubt his word."

"What do you say, Sergeant?" asked Weekes.

"I'm with the Captain, sir. I've observed his men—battle-hardened. They'll put up a good fight and should keep the Russians occupied long enough for the Captain and me to reach the mountain undetected. The local militia knows all the paths up to the plateau. They'll act as our guide."

"What then?" asked Weekes.

"We call in one of our drones," replied Drum. "With any luck, they'll activate their equipment. I'll capture the frequencies and take measurements. If we can, we'll destroy both the jammer and the SAMs."

Weekes frowned. "We'll be splitting up the troop—spreading ourselves thin."

"That's a risk, I agree," said Drum.

Weekes tapped his finger absentmindedly on the map. "But I don't have a better plan."

Brock smiled. "So it's a goer?"

"With a slight modification," said Weekes. "Cairns and McPherson will go with you. Cairns is a good man in a pinch and you'll need the explosives expertise of McPherson."

"I couldn't agree more," replied Drum. "But that will leave you thin on the ground when the party starts at this end."

Weekes nodded. "I'll need Prakash for comms and Davis will be put to good use as a sniper. It'll be Asadi's men that'll be the problem. Other than the girl, no one in the village speaks English. She'll have to stay with me and help coordinate the attack. What armaments do they have?"

"I've clocked one fifty-cal mounted on a flatbed; the usual assortment of RPG's; we have the GPMG and several rocket launchers," said Brock. "Should be enough to kick up a ruckus."

"It's agreed then," said Weekes. "Let's get everyone together and work out the detail. I have a feeling it's going to be a long night."

14

Harry stared at the computer screen in frustration. She'd spent the last two days rummaging around the Petrov Corporation's computer system looking for any signs of money laundering without success. She bit her lower lip and chided herself for her rash decision to take up Marchetti's offer. She'd need at least a year to find evidence of any money laundering scheme—even with an army of other forensic accountants. The problem was her limited access to the mainframe. She needed greater security clearance. That might mean taking up Petrov's many invitations for a night out on the town. Marchetti had been right. He was a sucker for redheads.

Her rope of copper-red hair had been her entry into the organisation —that and a shady introduction from one of Marchetti's crooked bankers. He'd provided Petrov with a glowing report of her skills at hiding money from the IRS and dropped pointed comments about her other assets. Marchetti seemed to know a lot of shady individuals. Petrov had hired her on the spot and she entered his organisation the very next day as an accountant in the real estate part of the business. What she knew of Manhattan real estate you could write on a postage stamp, but it was a way in.

"Penny for your thoughts?"

She looked up to see Jonathan standing at her desk. He was a tall, good-looking guy, about her age, with a pleasant lopsided smile and a mop of unruly blond hair. He had introduced himself on her first day in the department and had helped her settle in.

His co-worker was a different kettle of fish. Mandy was a short, plump woman, perhaps a few years older. It wasn't clear what Mandy did exactly—she wasn't part of the accounting team. She seemed to spend all her time dealing with insurance claims on the many properties that the Petrov Corporation owned in the city. Harry had tried several times to make small talk with the woman, but she snubbed her on every occasion.

Harry stopped chewing on her lip. "I guess I'm a little frustrated at finding my way around the computer system."

Jonathan smiled his lopsided smile and pulled up a chair next to her. She could feel Mandy's eyes boring into the back of her head.

"Here, let me help."

He slid his chair close to hers and leaned in to access her keyboard. He smelt of talcum and aftershave.

"OK, what is it you're trying to find?"

"Well, I'm trying to get a listing of the company properties—commercial and non-commercial—and any loans on the balance sheet."

Harry knew that criminals often loaned each other money to disguise illegal transfers of funds from law enforcement. She guessed this would be a good place to start.

"A listing of all properties shouldn't be a problem. You have access to that. Just run this query against the property database. The system uses Simple Query Language. Here, let me show you."

Jonathan ran his fingers over the keyboard and typed a long string of parameters into a field on the screen.

"I've typed out the SQL parameters for you." He hit the return button and a few seconds later a report scrolled up on the screen. "There you go." He typed a few more commands. "I've saved the query and named it 'Harry's Property Listing.' The next time you run the query, the system will send the report to your corporate email account."

"Wow! That's amazing. Thanks, Jonathan." She turned and flashed him her best smile. "What about the loans?"

He pushed his chair back and gave her a slight pout. "Can't help you there. We don't have access to that area of the accounts. Why are you interested anyway?"

She had come prepared for that question. "Tax avoidance." She was careful not to use the word 'evasion'. That would be illegal. Accountants—especially crooked ones—were sensitive to the nuances of their terminology.

"I see." He gave her a knowing look. "I suppose it's the reason you're here. Let me run it by the folks upstairs and get back to you."

"Jonathan, you're a brick!"

He frowned. "I'm a brick?"

She laughed. "Yes, sorry. I forget not all British slang crosses the pond. It means you're a kind person."

"You're welcome," he said. "Well, I'll leave you to it. I'm going downstairs for a break. Can I get anyone a coffee?"

"Thanks, Jonathan. I'll have a black Americano," said Harry.

"I'll come with you, Jonny," chimed in Mandy, jumping up and grabbing him by the arm. "I could do with a smoke."

"You guys have fun," said Harry smiling.

Mandy glared at her as they left the office.

Harry waited for the chime of the elevator and gave it a few more minutes before walking over to Mandy's desk. Her computer terminal was still active and her account logged in. She had observed the woman repeatedly leave her desk without ever logging out, relying on the system to time-out. Harry had noted that the system logged Mandy out after twenty minutes, which by security standards was very lax. IT had probably configured Mandy's terminal this way to stop her logging endless calls for password changes. An IT nightmare. Her work area confirmed Harry's suspicions. There were crumbs of food everywhere and her keyboard looked like it had caught the Black Death. She wished she'd brought rubber gloves.

Harry set a timer on her phone for twenty minutes and sat down at the terminal. She had plenty of time. Mandy would keep Jonathan talking for a good thirty minutes. She noted the screen Mandy was working on and entered the menu system. Mandy's menu options looked very different and more comprehensive than the menu presented on her terminal. This was because Mandy had greater security privileges. Harry knew that good computer security relied on giving people only the access they needed. And Mandy appeared to have a lot of access. Harry reasoned that the woman didn't need this level of security for dealing with insurance claims. She had probably worked on the system during its development and her high level of access had never been reviewed or revoked. It was a common security failing and the reason so many corporate systems were vulnerable to attack.

She found the area of the accounts system she was looking for. There were several standard reports already set up, including a breakdown of the company's balance sheet and its profit and loss. All standard fare. The detail of the balance sheet should contain the loans she was looking for. Delaney had given her access to a resource to help with the analysis. A guy called Jimmy Miller. She typed his email address into the reporting system. His external email account would receive all the reports she subsequently generated. She hoped the security of the corporate email system wasn't good enough to block the reports leaving the corporate domain. She then returned to Mandy's original screen.

On a hunch, she scrolled through the fields on the screen. Mandy was preparing a large claim for a property on the Lower Eastside of town. It ran to several million dollars. She noted the name of the property. An extensive cinema complex. From the look of the report Jonathan had just run on her terminal, there were many such properties.

I wonder, she thought. She looked at the time. She had ten minutes, at most, before Mandy returned to her cesspit of a desk. She brought up the reporting system and started to type in a customised SQL query. She needed a report linking all existing claims against her list of properties. Despite her protestations of ignorance to Jonathan, her skill at using SQL to interrogate a system was second to none.

She checked the time again on her phone and cursed. The query was taking longer to form than she had originally thought. The system's SQL was a little quirky. She tried several times to run the report, but each time it failed. The seconds relentlessly ticked down. She calmed herself and examined each parameter, character by character. Then she realised her mistake. She was using an American keyboard and had typed in the wrong character for the file descriptor: forward slash, not a backslash. She erased that part of the query and stabbed at the character on the keyboard, but nothing happened.

She heard the chime of the elevator announcing its arrival. The dulcet drone of Mandy's voice echoed down the corridor, dripping sarcasm.

"Oh, Jonathan. You're such a brick!"

Harry bit her lip and peered at the grimy keyboard. A fragment of a painted nail was wedged under the offending key. She held the keyboard upside down and gave it a good shake. Detritus rained down onto the floor along with the broken nail. Harry returned the keyboard to its place on the desk and finished the query.

Please keep him talking a little longer, thought Harry.

She stabbed the Enter button and prayed the report would run uninterrupted. She was out of time. She could hear the couple outside the door. She returned to Mandy's original screen and logged her out.

"Hey, we're back," said Jonathan, looking a little sheepish. "Sorry, we took so long. Big queue at the new coffee place." He handed Harry her coffee.

"We're back!" chimed Mandy, smirking as she returned to her pit.

"No problem," said Harry, from her desk. "Just going over the report."

"Damn," said Mandy "I've been logged out."

Harry turned to see her peering at a post-it note in her drawer. She stabbed at a few keys and logged back into the system, carrying on where she had left off.

"Thanks for the coffee," said Harry, grateful for a break. "My treat next time."

"You're on," said Jonathan, smiling.

"Hey!" cried Mandy. "IT has finally fixed my keyboard".

15

Harry had been sitting in the small coffee shop just off Bryant Park for over an hour. She'd agreed to meet Delaney's man, Jimmy Miller, there, but the guy was late. She was on her third Americano; any more and she'd be climbing the walls. The dregs of a good night's sleep sloshed around in the bottom of her cup.

Miller was one of Delaney's recent hires. Originally from Boston, he'd only moved to New York just over a week ago. It was one reason she had come all the way uptown to Delaney's Midtown office. It should have taken him only a few minutes to walk from the black monolith of an office on 47th and Sixth to the park.

A tall, lean young man entered the shop and scanned the room. She hoped to God it was Miller. He was casually dressed, sporting a brown leather jacket over a plain, white t-shirt. Harry admired the snug fit of his tailored blue jeans that narrowed down at the ankles to a pair of white trainers. She wondered if all of Delaney's analysts dressed this way for the office.

"You must be Harriet."

"You must be Jimmy—and call me Harry."

Jimmy Millar pulled up a chair and sat down. "Sorry I'm late. I lost track of time."

Harry waited for him to continue the conversation, but he just sat there gazing at her with his grey-blue eyes. He had a youthful, animated face that was framed by a shock of unruly black hair which he wore long to the collar.

"Well, at least you found me," said Harry, trying to break the ice.

"Oh, it wasn't hard. A beautiful young woman with a rope of copper-coloured hair."

"If that's supposed to be a line, I'm not in the mood. I've been waiting for over an hour and I'm tired and hungry—"

"Sorry, it wasn't a line. It's how Delaney described you."

"Oh, right. Sorry, I'm a little snappy from drinking all this coffee."

Jimmy gave her a quizzical look as if trying to decipher some deeper social meaning to the situation. His face softened into a smile.

"I'm not very good around people, I'm afraid. More of a numbers person. I've upset you."

Delaney had mentioned this in passing.

"I'm lending you Jimmy Miller," she'd said. "He's our best analyst. He has a gift with numbers."

She relaxed a little. "I'm not upset, Jimmy. Just tired. What have you got for me? I don't see a laptop."

"I carried out a quick analysis of your data this morning once I received your email. I'll send you my full findings in a report for future reference."

"You don't have it with you," said Harry, annoyed that she had nothing to show for her long wait.

"No, it would have taken too long and Delaney said you needed it in a hurry. I printed out the data and scanned it. The results are pretty conclusive."

"Wait, you printed out the data … but there must be over a hundred pages?"

"A hundred and twenty-six."

"And you scanned them?"

"Yes, I laid them out on the floor and looked for correlations. It will all be in the report."

"I don't understand," said Harry. "You laid them out on the floor? You didn't run an analytics program against the data?"

Jimmy smiled. "It sounds weird, I know. But it's what I do. Delaney calls it a gift. I can't explain it. I'll put it in the final report. It'll stand up in court, don't worry."

"Sounds bonkers," said Harry, but was too tired to argue.

"Bonkers? Is that like your British 'Bollocks'?"

Harry burst out laughing. "Similar, Jimmy. Just give me the skinny."

Jimmy's face softened as he relaxed into the situation. She guessed he found social situations awkward. Once more his eyes drew her in.

"Basically, they're operating an insurance scam. Your hunch was right."

"Mad Mandy," mused Harry.

"Who?"

It was her turn to smile. "Nothing, Jimmy. How does it work?"

"Petrov buys up large numbers of worthless properties. He may even get some public subsidy for developing the sites. He then buys insurance on each property, paying hefty premiums. From my quick analysis of the data, he waits a year, then cancels the policy and sells the property. He may even claim against some larger ones—there're numerous claims for fire damage and loss."

"The cinema complex on the Lower Eastside," added Harry.

"That's one example." Jimmy looked around. "I'm starving."

Harry realised she was hungry too. "We'll grab a bite later. What else?"

"Well, there is a large loan on the books. Didn't have time to trace it, but I'm sure you'll find it's being used to pay for the premiums. When the policy is cancelled the insurer will refund a good percentage of the money. The money is now clean, and the cycle continues. I estimate they're making seventy-five cents on the dollar."

Harry beamed. "Great work, Jimmy."

"You really are a beautiful woman."

Harry frowned.

"That *was* a line," said Jimmy.

16

It was midday when the insertion team reached the base of the plateau. Abdul had decided that he would be both driver and navigator. Drum had winced as the Land Rover's engine whined in protest over the several klicks of the journey. Apparently, the use of gears was optional in the militia.

So far so good, thought Drum. They got out and pulled their kit from the back of the Land Rover. Because of the climb, Brock had decided that they would carry minimal equipment in their Bergens. It was still a heavy load with the addition of sixty metres of rope and climbing tackle. Drum had insisted that they leave their standard-issue personal radios in the vehicle. Radio silence was paramount until the diversionary attack had begun. They gathered some loose shrubs and did their best to camouflage the Land Rover with the sparse vegetation from the surrounding area. It wouldn't pass close inspection but was good enough if viewed from a distance.

The path Hamid had chosen for the climb was barely discernible—a narrow, meandering track that led steeply upwards. It would be tough in the sun's heat.

Brock looked up in despair. "You must be joking."

Cairns barely concealed his laughter and Hazard grinned.

"Bottle it you two," barked Brock.

Drum regarded his friend, a little surprised. "Didn't know you were scared of heights?"

"I ain't scared," protested Brock. "Just cautious with all the gear we're carrying. And if you fall, this entire operation will have been a complete waste of time."

"It's not Drum you need to worry about," said Hazard. "With all the explosives I'm carrying, one slip and the whole mountain will come down on top of us."

"Fucking marvellous," muttered Brock.

Abdul spoke impatiently to Hamid, who nodded and tugged on Drum's arm.

"Time to go, chaps," said Drum, and started up the narrow path in the footsteps of their young guide.

They struck a good pace with the men keeping up with Hamid. Drum considered it amusing that their mission rested entirely upon the shoulders of this twelve-year-old boy. Their pace slowed after an hour as the track narrowed even further and the men formed up in single file with Abdul bringing up the rear. Occasionally, the man would bark some order resulting in the boy turning to Drum, gesturing to him to move faster.

"Fuck me," said Brock, "if he barks one more time I swear I'll throw him off this mountain myself." He turned and gave Abdul the evil eye. Abdul merely shrugged and waved him forward.

After two hours into the back-breaking climb, the path all but disappeared.

"Blimey," said Brock. "Are you sure he knows the way?"

Drum looked down at the sheer vertical wall of rock falling away below him. In the distance, the vista of the valley shimmered in a heat haze. Brock was right: one slip and they would be off the edge. He tapped Hamid on the shoulder. The boy turned. Drum held out his hands and drew them in: too narrow.

Hamid shook his head and pointed up ahead. He indicated that they would be turning. He then held his arms out wide.

"I hope he means the path will get wider," said Brock.

Drum looked behind him to see how the rest of the men were doing. It was a mistake. The bulk of his Bergen hit the side of the rock and pushed him sideways. His foot slipped over the edge and he flailed for a hand-hold. Rock and shingle cascaded over the side and down the mountain. In desperation, he turned back to face the track just as a meaty hand and a strong arm pushed him against the rock face.

"Don't do that, Captain," said Brock. "I didn't bring a change of underwear."

The rest of the men laughed.

"I just realised," said Drum, panting. "We can't turn back."

The laughing stopped.

Abdul shouted an order from the back of the line and Hamid

continued on.

It was another thirty minutes before they hit the turn. Drum dripped with sweat. He could hear the ragged breathing of the men behind him. As promised, the track suddenly grew wider, giving each man more room to manoeuvre. Drum realised that they had entered the hollow of a dried-up waterfall. He imagined a torrent of water falling from some natural spring above, carving a vertical gully in the sheer rock face before disappearing over the edge. He licked his lips. They must be close to the top of the plateau.

The track transformed into a wide ledge that looked out onto the valley below. At the back of the ledge Drum could just make out the entrance to a cave in the shadows of the rock face. At least it was somewhere they could stop and rest, he thought.

Hamid led them to the cave and sat down. Each man wearily removed the load from his back and slumped down in the cool of the shade.

"I hope this is the end of the line," said Brock. He removed his water bottle from his belt and took a long drink of water. Each man did the same. Drum gulped down several mouthfuls before handing his bottle to Hamid. The boy nodded his thanks and drank a little of the water before handing the bottle back.

"What now?" said Hazard. "Weekes will kick off the attack soon."

"I don't know about you lot," said Charming, "but I'm going to take a leak." He disappeared into the depths of the cave.

Drum looked at his watch. Thirty minutes before the attack started. "We need to get set up. Charming can catch us up."

He tapped Hamid on the shoulder, then tapped his watch. The boy nodded and beckoned to the men to follow.

They moved out of the cool of the cave and back into the heat of the sun. Hamid scampered along the ledge which receded into the rock face before twisting around an overhanging outcrop of rock, which made the path impassable from that point on.

Hamid beckoned to them to get down on their hands and knees. They crawled to the bend in the path, just below the overhang, and looked down over the ledge. Directly below them was a broad, flat plateau of rock, the size of two football fields. Drum noticed a smooth, wide road leading off the plateau at the far end. It looked well maintained and descended to the valley below. Someone's been busy.

Parked close to the edge of the plateau was a large, six-wheeled truck, decked out in military olive-green. A tall mast rose from a hatch in the back, stabilised on each side by several tethers fastened to the hard granite rock. Parked close by was a smaller trailer, with four similar masts attached to each of its corners and connected to the truck by a long snaking cable.

"I think we've found your comms array," said Brock. He put a meaty hand on Hamid's head and mussed up his hair. Abdul gave the boy a toothy grin.

"I estimate about forty to fifty metres to the bottom," said Hazard. "We have just enough rope to abseil down."

Drum cast an expert eye over the equipment. "This is it. A Russian Kvant, designed for ECM. It has a powerful transmitter, pumping out sizeable amounts of energy in the Ku-band of frequencies."

"What does that mean in English?" asked Brock.

"And can we blow it up?" added Hazard.

Drum grinned. "It's designed for Electronic Counter Measures. It's why we can't use our radios. They're probably tracking all comms over a wide range of frequencies. And the transmitter—that will seriously fuck up any radar. We can't destroy it until I've monitored the frequency it's transmitting on."

"Is this the reason our drones don't work in this area?" asked Hazard.

"Maybe," said Drum. He pulled out his field glasses and inspected the masts. "Yes, the larger of the masts coming out of the main vehicle has an unusual configuration. I suspect it's spoofing the GPS signal."

"Screwing with the drone's position," added Hazard.

"Right," said Drum. "We'll know for sure once Weekes calls in the drone." He looked at his watch. He had minutes to prepare his equipment. "I'd better get cracking."

Abdul pointed to the back of the plateau. Three Taliban fighters appeared, flanking a man dressed in fatigues. A technician, thought Drum. The man sauntered to the truck and disappeared into the back. The three fighters stood guard outside.

"Where did they come from?" said Brock.

Drum leaned further over the edge. "Here, grab my feet."

Brock and Hazard each grabbed a leg. Drum pushed himself further off the ledge, suspending his upper body in mid-air. He bent at the waist to see under the overhang.

"Bloody hell. How did we miss those?"

"What do you see?" asked Brock, panting with exertion.

"Two bloody great blast doors, set into the rock face. There must be a large cave system back there. Pull me up." The two soldiers heaved Drum back onto the ledge.

"I'll bet a month's wages that's where they're storing the SAM's," said Brock.

"Either way, we need to crack on," said Drum. "Hang on, where's Charming?"

"He must still be back at the cave," said Hazard. "Silly bugger probably wandered in too far and got lost."

There was silence as the realisation sunk in.

"Fuck it, let's go back and look for the idiot," said Brock.

They scrambled back along the path until it was wide enough for them to stand. They jogged back to the cave entrance.

"His gear is still here," said Drum.

"Charming!" shouted Brock into the mouth of the cave. His voice echoed and reverberated against the rocky walls.

Abdul grabbed Brock by the arm and put his finger to his mouth. Quiet.

Brock angrily pulled his arm away.

Hamid tugged at Drum's sleeve and pointed down into the valley. A flare hung in the air above the village.

They were out of time.

17

Major Timothy Weekes watched his flare arc high over the centre of the enemy compound, a bright red jewel against the deepening blue of the Afghan sky. That should get their attention. He threw the spent pistol into the back of the Land Rover and jumped behind the wheel. In the passenger seat next to him, Aisha clutched one of the troop's military radios in a trembling hand. She watched wide-eyed as the flare danced and spiralled on its descent, trailing a plume of white smoke in its wake.

Weekes started the engine and turned to Anil Prakash hunched over the radio in the back of the vehicle. "Order up the drone, Corporal. Tell HQ the attack has commenced."

"Roger that, Major." Prakash ran his hand deftly over the radio dials and tuned to a specific frequency. "Big Bear, this is Grey Wolf, receiving?"

A voice from the radio answered immediately and in a broad Glaswegian accent.

"Receiving Grey Wolf, Lima Charlie."

"Roger, Big Bear. Requesting eyes in the sky. Commencing attack."

"Roger, Grey Wolf. Eyes in the sky confirmed en-route." There was the slightest of pauses from the Glaswegian on the other end of the radio. "Good hunting. Big Bear out."

McKay, thought Weekes. Regardless of what people thought of the man, he was never one to sit behind a desk. The Scotsman always liked to be in the thick of things. He looked over at the shaking Aisha, her eyes wide with trepidation. He tapped the radio with his finger. "Asadi, attack."

Aisha clutched the radio in both hands and screamed a litany of

Pashto into the mic. An explosion ripped through the side of the compound, followed by bursts of gunfire from the surrounding rooftops. Asadi had joined the fray. Drummond was right, thought Weekes. This man was a force to be reckoned with. He slammed the Land Rover into gear.

"Time we moved, I think. They will have tracked our comms by now. Let's get to higher ground and make sure they don't outflank us." He floored the accelerator. "Hang on, Corporal."

The Land Rover leapt forward, kicking up a cloud of dust in its wake. Weekes planned to scoot around the outskirts of the village and head for higher ground where he could direct the attack. They sped past deserted mud shelters, running parallel to an irrigation canal. Up ahead, the village mosque loomed above the smaller dwellings.

"Roof of the mosque," shouted Weekes. "RPG."

Prakash clambered onto the rear machine gun and sighted on a lone figure with a shoulder-mounted RPG. He racked the gun's mechanism and fired off several bursts as best he could as the vehicle bounced along the rocky track. The mosque exterior exploded around the insurgent, but not before he loosed a round. Weekes heard the familiar whooshing sound as the deadly rocket-propelled grenade passed less than a metre overhead and exploded in the cornfield on the other side of the ditch. Prakash let rip with another burst of gunfire as they passed the mosque, peppering the fighter into a bloody mess before the fatal rounds threw him off the wall.

"Good shooting, Corporal."

Weekes kept his foot to the floor as they raced along the track. Another explosion shook the ground and a column of smoke rose from a smaller compound on their right. Then he heard it. The distinctive sound of a 50-cal machine gun. The familiar chattering of the weapon grew closer. Up ahead the road narrowed and funnelled them down a narrow street. Weekes slowed. This was not looking good. A flat-bed truck suddenly appeared from a side street and skidded to a halt, blocking their path. Mounted on the back was the 50-cal and it was turning their way.

18

The distant sound of an explosion echoed down the valley. Drum scrambled to assemble his gear close to the edge of the overhang. Hamid squatted down beside him, watching intently. He had left the rest of the team searching the cave system for Charming. Soldiers of the SAS don't just wander off and Drum had a bad feeling about the cave.

He pulled equipment from his pack and worked quickly on the final assembly of the GCHQ monitoring device. His days of preparation were finally paying off. He extended a small portable antenna and connected it to a frequency analyser. He plugged this into his laptop and ran a specially written program. The system burst into life and the familiar trace of a jamming signal bounced across the screen. It confirmed his suspicions. Two distinct frequencies, emulating the L1 and L2 carrier waves of a GPS signal, were being transmitted by the array at significant power. He pressed record and waited.

A grinding sound came up from the plateau below. Drum pressed his face to the rocky path and squinted under the overhang. The blast doors were opening. Two jeeps appeared, filled with men in Afghan dress but looking distinctly like soldiers. Spetsnaz, thought Drum. They have a history of disguising themselves as insurgents to cover their tracks.

The two jeeps took off along the roadway, heading down into the valley. The diversion was working. He looked at his screen. His analyser was happily recording the data he needed. Time to find the rest of the team. He grabbed his pack and tapped Hamid on the shoulder. They crawled back along the path until they could stand and run back to the mouth of the cave.

There was no sign of the troop.

He dropped his gear and checked inside the cave entrance. He stood still and waited for his eyes to adjust to the gloom. He strained to hear any sound but there was nothing except the occasional splash of water dripping from the roof of the cave.

Hamid waved Drum over. The boy had found two packs of gear carefully stowed against one wall. He knelt and inspected both packs. One belonged to Hazard. Drum recognised the small, red patch sewn onto the side pocket. The man had decided against carrying his explosives into the cave. The other pack belonged to Charming. As far as he could tell, no one had disturbed the contents of either pack. He stepped further into the mouth of the cave. He curbed the urge to shout, mindful of Abdul's prior warning. As his eyes adjusted to the darkness, he could make out the glow of a red flare. Dropped by the team, he reasoned. He checked the clip of his Browning and turned to Hamid.

"Wait here, Hamid." He pointed at the ground.

Hamid was having none of it. He grabbed Drum by the arm and shook his head. He was coming too. Drum didn't have time to argue. He nodded and moved to find his pack. The boy stuck to him like glue.

"Don't like the dark," he mused, but knew the boy didn't understand. "They're in here somewhere."

He found his pack and fished out a flashlight and a length of rope. Each man had brought a standard sixty metres and he wasn't prepared to leave his behind. He repacked the rope in Hazard's Bergen and shouldered the load. He didn't like the idea of leaving the explosives unguarded. He turned on his flashlight and they moved deeper into the cave.

The cave quickly forked into several smaller caves connected by narrow, twisting tunnels that led this way and that. Flares had been left at intervals. Without them, they had no hope of finding their way out. Here and there, large pools of water had formed on the floor. They looked like large mirrors reflecting the eery, red glow of the flares. It reminded Drum of the time he'd gone caving in Wales with one of the army's survival instructors. An old guy by the name of Jeffries. He'd given them a stark warning: 'don't tread in the water, lads. They may look like puddles but can be large wells, many metres deep. Step in and you'll sink like a stone without a trace.' He hoped the rest of the team had attended the same course.

Drum noticed that the flares were now more widely spaced out. The search team must be down to their last few. The way ahead narrowed and he felt the tunnel close in. The walls of the passage ran wet with trickles of moisture and there was a strange smell in the air which grew stronger the deeper they penetrated the cave. Hamid could smell it too. He wrinkled his nose and coughed. Drum suddenly realised what it was: exhaust fumes.

He pulled off his scarf and wet it on the wall of the tunnel. He gave it to Hamid and helped the boy tie it over his mouth and nose. He took a bandana from his pocket and did the same. They pressed on further into the cave system.

Drum was feeling dizzy. He suspected what might have happened to Charming. He hoped the rest of the men had had the good sense to turn back or seek another exit, but the flares continued.

It was getting warmer and Drum's head was starting to pound. Carbon monoxide poisoning, he told himself. He could hear a rhythmical chugging sound up ahead. It had to be a diesel generator. The flares suddenly came to an end as they rounded a bend. He heard voices and then the generator suddenly stopped. Drum drew his weapon and moved cautiously forward. Up ahead he could see a dim pulsing light. Hamid suddenly slumped to his knees. He picked up the boy in his arms and started to turn back. One by one the flares began to splutter and die. Too late, that route was now closed. He hefted the boy over his shoulder and carried him quickly towards the light.

Manoeuvres

19

Weekes brought the Land Rover skidding to a halt. The flat-bed truck with its 50-cal machine gun had completely cut them off. The narrow street had boxed them in with nowhere to run.

"Light him up," shouted Weekes.

Prakash racked back on the mounted machine gun and sighted down on the flat-bed. He let loose a sustained volley of 7.62mm rounds, peppering the cab and shredding the driver. The broken body fell forward onto the steering column, setting the horn in a mournful wailing. The barrel of the GPMG hissed and smoked white-hot from the sustained burst, preventing the weapon from firing.

Weekes stepped calmly down from behind the wheel and reached for a storage locker mounted on the side of the Land Rover. The insurgent on the 50-cal had fallen back off his weapon from the hail of bullets hitting his vehicle, buying them some time, but the armour surrounding the weapon had saved the man. He would soon return fire.

Weekes unloaded an M72 LAW Rocket Launcher, courtesy of their American friends. He'd been a corporal the last time he'd fired one, but it was a simple device the size of a small, green drainpipe. Like riding a bike, he reassured himself. He flipped off the front cover and tugged on the back, which extended the tube, causing two sights to flip up. He stood, legs braced, and shouldered the weapon. The gunner on the flat-bed had now recovered from their previous salvo and was racking back on the 50-cal.

"Better get clear, Corporal," said Weekes, closing one eye and sighting along the LAW's tube.

Weekes slid his fingers around the smooth metal tube until he felt the rubber cover of the firing mechanism. He tried to concentrate as Prakash cursed in Nepalese and struggled to unfreeze the red-hot weapon, determined to get off another burst. He pressed down on the trigger and braced for the launch of the rocket, but all he heard was the clattering sound of the 50-cal, echoing off the walls of the street.

Weekes pressed the rubber button again and again, but the LAWs failed to fire. What had he forgotten?

Pillars of dirt erupted from the street as the 50-cal traced a deadly line of destruction towards them. Weekes dropped the LAWs and grabbed Aisha from her seat as the wall beside her exploded into fragments of mud and dust from the 50-cal rounds. Prakash cried out and fell from the back of the Land Rover onto the dirt road. He lay there, unmoving, his chest a bloody mess.

The insurgent had zeroed in on their position and was racking back on the 50-cal to finish them off when the sound of a high-velocity round split the air with a high-pitched whine. Travelling at nearly supersonic speed, the large Magnum round found its target with pinpoint accuracy. The insurgent's head exploded, throwing the decapitated corpse over the side of the vehicle.

Weekes heard the soft, West Country accent of Poacher over his comms. "Sorry I'm late, Major."

Weekes tapped his headset. "Thank you, Corporal." He hesitated. "Prakash didn't make it."

There was a pause in comms. "Sorry to hear that. He was a good soldier."

Yes, he was, thought Weekes. But why didn't that bloody LAWs fire?

He picked up the half-cocked rocket launcher from the street and examined it. Almost at once he realised his stupidity. He'd forgotten to take off the safety. That mistake had cost Prakash his life.

Weekes mentally shook himself and dropped the weapon. He needed to reassure his men and keep the attack moving. They needed to find a way out of this maze of streets.

"Poacher, can you find me a way out of here?"

"Yes, Major. Reverse half a klick. There's a side road on your left. That should lead you out to the fields."

"Roger that."

There was a squawking from the radio in the back of Land Rover. Aisha ran over and grabbed the headset and receiver. She fumbled with the equipment and nodded several times before acknowledging the transmission verbally in Pashto. She turned to Weekes.

"Asadi say men from the mountain are coming this way."

He nodded. The diversion had worked. Weekes looked down at the bloody body of Prakash. They had played their hand and it had cost them dear. Now it was up to Drummond to play his.

20

Drum staggered to the end of the tunnel under the weight of Hamid and Hazard's explosive laden pack. He had placed the small flashlight between his teeth to free up his gun hand and hoped to God that no one fired at him: one hit to Hazard's pack and the entire mountain would come down on top of them. He rounded the corner, gun extended and stopped in his tracks.

He'd entered a small cavern lined with wall lights, which were now fading to a dim orange glow. In the far corner sat a small generator, its ignition light slowly pulsing. Someone had just turned it off and the last of its charge was draining fast. In the centre of the cavern, a bright square of light broke through the dark, wet floor, illuminating a half-opened hatch. Drum played his light around the rest of the interior. Two bodies lay slumped against one wall. They looked to be sleeping.

He staggered forward, stooping almost to his knees, and placed Hamid gently on the floor. He walked over to the bodies and shone his light over the faces of the two men. They were local, probably from the village. The paler of their skin was a sickly cherry red. Carbon monoxide poisoning. The generator had killed them.

A waft of cool, fresh air came up through the hatch. Drum walked carefully around it and back to Hamid. He dragged the boy close to the opening and checked his pulse. It was weak but steady. He hoped the fresh air would revive him. Drum squatted and peered down into the void. A familiar voice drifted up from the cavern below.

"You took your fucking time," whispered Brock.

Drum was too tired to reply with a smart remark. Brock was standing beside a lowered cherry picker with the rest of the troop gathered around him. It's probably how the two local men had accessed the hatch. Their mistake had been closing it while the generator was on. His head continued to pound.

"Raise the cradle," whispered Drum.

Brock jumped onto the platform of the cherry picker and worked the controls. A whining noise started from inside the main chassis of the vehicle and the scissor-like supports beneath the cage extended. It took a full minute for the platform to reach the top of the hatch.

"He all right?" asked Brock, pointing to Hamid.

"The fumes got to him," said Drum. "He should be all right once we get him out of here."

The two men slid the small boy onto the platform. He was already beginning to stir. Drum grabbed the rest of his gear and lowered it gently onto the cradle.

"Is that what I think it is?" said Brock, smiling.

Drum nodded. "Hazard's bag of tricks."

"He may well get to use them," said Brock. "We hit the jackpot."

Brock quickly worked the controls on the cradle and they descended. A groan came up from below. Charming had his arm around Abdul and was limping badly. He gave up trying to walk and sat back down on the floor. He cursed loudly.

"What happened?" asked Drum.

"Bit of a balls up, really. We guessed Charming had got himself lost, so we started a search. It soon became clear that the cave system was extensive—hence the flares. We found him unconscious at the entrance to the narrow tunnel that leads into the maintenance area above. It's there we heard the generator. The plan was to get Charming back outside—we were all feeling the effects of the fumes—but he weighs a ton ..."

"So you pressed on ahead," said Drum.

"Right. Didn't have much of a choice. We stumbled upon those poor buggers—killed themselves by closing the hatch. Abdul recognised them from the village. He was none too pleased."

"But what happened to Charming?" asked Drum.

"Well, we opens the hatch and sees the cherry picker right there. Brilliant, we thought. So we try to lower Charming into the cradle ..."

"But?"

"We dropped him."

"You dropped him?"

"Right. Clumsy, I know. But as I said, he ain't no lightweight. Lands badly on his foot—we think he's broken his ankle."

"It might have been better if you'd dropped him on his head," said Drum.

Brock nodded in agreement. "Right, no chance of doing any damage."

The cherry picker whined to a halt. They appeared to be inside a spacious, well-lit cavern. Drum estimated they had descended about twenty metres from the hatch above. All around them, large generators and ventilation systems hummed with the exertion of powering the base and keeping fresh air circulating. They were inside a gigantic generator room. It must have taken a small army to complete a project of this size and complexity, he thought. At the far end of the room, Abdul stood sentry at a set of large, steel doors. His brow creased with concern when he saw Hamid stretched out on the cradle of the cherry picker.

Drum picked up the boy and sat him up next to Charming. He was already starting to wake up in the fresh circulating air.

Drum laid a comforting hand on the shoulder of the despondent corporal. "How you doing, mate."

"Sorry, Cap. I fucked up."

"Nonsense. You found us a way in."

Charming smiled. "Right. You could say that."

"Can you walk?"

"Only with a bit of help. The ankle's knackered."

Drum looked up at the hatch. Even with the cherry picker, getting Charming out that way was a big ask—and that's if they could find their way out through the maze of tunnels without the help of the flares. They had to find another exit.

Hazard walked over with his bag of explosives. "Glad you brought these." What's the plan, Captain?"

Until now, Drum's only concern had been keeping Hamid alive. He hadn't planned on being inside the facility. He looked around the enormous space filled with the whine and hum of large machinery. Well-placed explosives would cripple the facility, but getting out would be a different matter. He looked down at Hamid. The boy was now sitting up and looking better. How would he fare in a fire-fight? He turned to Brock, looking for inspiration.

"It's your call, Captain," said Brock. "We're stuck between a rock and a hard place if we stay here. The only other exit is through those doors. Leads to a passage of some sorts. Might be the way out."

Drum looked down at Charming, who was wincing in pain. His

ankle looked swollen.

"Corporal?"

Charming spat on the floor. "Fuck it. I say we blow the place. I'll make it. Don't worry about me."

Drum pointed to the bag of explosives. "Can we trigger an explosion remotely once we're outside?"

"Unlikely," replied Hazard. "We're too far inside the mountain. It'll block any signal."

"Timer?"

"Sixty minutes, max."

Drum looked up at the hatch. "Well, we can't go back. We'd risk getting lost and the mountain coming down on top of us. We can't stay here—"

"And we can't surrender," added Brock. "Not to the Taliban."

There was no simple choice. "We blow the place. We'll make our escape the best we can," said Drum.

"Right then," said Hazard. "I'll give us the full sixty minutes."

21

It took Hazard less than fifteen minutes to plant his explosives. Drum watched as he expertly fused and placed each device. A total of four packages. He spread them around the generator room, placing them under key equipment, and then attached a final device under a large tank of diesel.

"All set, Captain. Sixty minutes and counting," said Hazard.

Drum set his watch. The clock was ticking.

"Ammo count," commanded Drum.

Each man checked their weapon and the magazines in their webbing. Drum had only two spare clips for his Browning. He hoped it would be enough.

Abdul was waving.

Drum moved quickly over to the door, joined by Brock. Abdul shaped his hand into a gun, then walked his fingers towards them. They had visitors. Drum peered between the two doors that Abdul had left slightly ajar. An unarmed technician in fatigues was coming their way, followed by an armed insurgent. The technician paused beside a sturdy steel door, inset into the passageway a few metres from their position. The technician checked a clipboard, unlocked the door and disappeared into a side room. The insurgent stood sentry outside. Drum moved back to Hamid and Charming.

"Armed guard just outside. Time to move, Corporal."

Charming used his rifle to push himself up from the floor and tried to put weight on his foot. He cried out in pain.

"Fuck it. Give me a hand, Hazard."

Hazard shouldered his Bergen and put his arm around Charming.

"C'mon mate," said Hazard. "Let's get you up." They took cover behind a packing crate of machine parts.

Drum knelt quickly beside Hamid and pulled him to his feet.

"Ok?"

The boy nodded. He was none the worse for wear. He pushed him behind a generator and squatted down beside him. He drew his weapon and chambered a round.

They heard a shout outside the door. Drum could just make out a few words of Russian over the hum of the generators. Charming's cry of pain had not gone undetected. The door creaked open and the insurgent stepped through, gun raised.

Before anyone could react, Abdul stepped out from behind the door and drew his knife. The insurgent cursed loudly and tried to bring his weapon to bear, but Abdul was too quick. He slammed into the man with his shoulder and grabbed the barrel of his rifle, forcing it down towards the floor. He smiled grimly as he drew his blade slowly across the man's throat. The insurgent went down with a gargled cry, but not before raking the floor with a burst of gunfire.

Bullets from the gun ricocheted loudly in the cavern's space. Somewhere behind Drum a pipe burst, gushing steam. Time to move.

Brock peered around the open door as the technician stepped out from the side room armed with an AK47. Brock grabbed Abdul and pulled him away from the door as a burst of gunfire raked the passageway. Bullets ricocheted off the floor and walls, just missing the two men. The noise from the weapon was deafening and the passageway filled with the smoke and the acrid smell of cordite.

Drum fired twice, one shot hitting the man in the gut. He doubled over, clutching his stomach. Brock stepped out and finished him with a single shot to the head. Abdul nodded his thanks to Brock.

"Let's move, people," said Drum.

Abdul picked up the insurgent's weapon and checked the magazine, then slammed it back in the stock. He spat as he stepped over the dead man.

Drum moved from behind the generator, dragging Hamid with him. Hazard and Charming were up and moving, albeit slowly, with Charming resting heavily on Hazard's shoulder. Drum knew it would be tough.

Drum caught up with Brock and Abdul outside the generator room. The passageway was well lit and wide enough for two abreast. It curved gently about twenty metres ahead of them with the bend obscuring its end. Two steel doors punctuated either side of the passageway. The technician lay outside the open door of a small room on their left, his body pooling blood on the rough concrete floor.

Hamid stared down wide-eyed at the bloodied corpse as they approached. Drum felt sorry for the boy. One minute he'd been herding goats and now he was in the middle of a life and death fire-fight in a man-made bunker under a mountain.

Abdul strode up and kicked the corpse. Drum didn't know why. The man was clearly dead. But for Abdul the act was personal. The death of the two villagers in the maintenance area above had been a blow. He bent down and picked up the dead man's AK. He looked down at Hamid and handed him the weapon.

"He'll end up shooting himself," said Brock, shaking his head.

Abdul quickly showed the boy how to charge the rifle, racking back on the slider. The AK47 was a simple weapon to fire. The boy reluctantly held the rifle. Abdul placed a hand on his shoulder and spoke softly to him. The boy nodded and raised his weapon. He was no longer a simple goat herder, but a fighter of the militia.

A klaxon sounded up ahead.

"Move it," said Brock. "They'll be here any minute."

Drum stepped over the dead technician, raised his weapon and entered the open door. It was a small storeroom filled with crates of machine parts and a rack of small arms, but otherwise empty.

"Clear!" he shouted.

He stepped back into the passageway and joined Brock at the second door. The door's signage was in Russian, but its bright yellow markings displayed the international symbol for flammable material.

Brock tried the handle. It opened with a satisfying click. He pushed the heavy door and peered inside, gun raised.

"Clear!"

Drum entered and surveyed the room. It was a much larger space and filled with barrels marked with the same flammable symbol. He poked his head outside of the door.

"Hazard. See what you can do with this."

Hazard gently rested Charming against the wall and walked over with his Bergen. He looked around the room and smiled.

"Leave it to me."

The team moved stealthily down the corridor with Drum and Brock leading. Abdul slung his arm around Charming and the two men shuffled behind. Hamid stuck close to Drum. He hoped the boy didn't accidentally shoot him in the arse.

They had reached the start of the bend when Drum heard footsteps. He raised his hand, and the group pushed themselves against the side of the passageway. Two guards came into view and halted in surprise. Brock let rip, raking the two men with automatic fire. The two men dropped to the floor in a bloody heap, the walls ringing loudly with the retorts of weapons fire.

"Move, move," urged Brock. "We can't get caught here."

They heard footsteps behind them. Hazard ran up, carrying his Bergen.

"That should make a nice bang. Just don't be around when it blows."

"How long?" asked Drum.

Roughly the same time as the ones in the generator room."

Charming winced in pain. "Roughly!"

"Well, give or take a few minutes."

Drum looked at his watch. Time had ticked by. Forty-five minutes left. "Let's go!"

They rounded the bend, guns raised, expecting to meet more resistance. Up ahead the passageway continued for another ten metres before ending at the entrance to a huge central cavern. They paused at the end of the passageway and pressed themselves close to the wall.

Drum peered into the gigantic space. It looked to be an enormous maintenance area with a smooth concrete floor and several work areas. High above them, a bright yellow gantry crane spanned the roof space. Suspended from the crane's central winch hung the sleek white body of an S400 surface-to-air missile. The missile swayed precariously a few metres above its mobile launch vehicle—a blocky, four-wheeled behemoth of a truck fitted with four missile tubes in pairs, two tubes atop each other, and decked out in desert camouflage. They had emerged at the tail-end of the vehicle and were looking down the length of four tubes. Three of the tubes were primed with missiles and the fourth was empty.

"Looks like we found the SAMs," said Brock. He looked up at the swaying missile. "Must have interrupted their loading".

Twenty metres directly in front of the vehicle were the two closed blast doors. They looked massive from inside the cavern.

Drum nodded toward the doors. "Our way out, but getting them open is another problem. I can't see any mechanism or control point."

Brock pointed up and to their right. "Up there. That raised housing. Stairs leading up. Looks like some form of control room."

Drum studied the housing, high on its platform overlooking the mobile launcher. It looked like a modified cargo container. Two technicians sat behind a long window which provided an unobstructed view of the maintenance area below. One technician stood and stared down at him.

"I'm betting that's where we'll find the controls for the blast doors," said Drum. "And they've spotted us."

Brock nodded. "That's our objective then."

A burst of gunfire erupted from their left. Bullets strafed the floor in front of them, sending up shards of concrete and dust before ricocheting off the passageway wall.

Abdul cursed loudly and clutched his arm. Blood trickled down his hand and dripped onto the floor.

"Where did they come from?" exclaimed Brock.

Hazard stepped forward and opened up with a burst of gunfire on full auto.

"Ten o'clock," he shouted. "Another tunnel on our left. At least eight tangos."

They were pinned down. Drum checked his watch. Thirty-five minutes until detonation.

22

Gunfire from the second group of insurgents tore up the concrete floor in front of the team. Loud, metallic clangs echoed around the cavern as bullets ricocheted off the missile tubes on the launcher and the suspended SAM, sending it spinning back and forth.

An angry Russian voice sounded over a loudspeaker system. The gunfire abruptly stopped.

"What was that all about?" said Brock, changing his magazine.

"Stop shooting at the very dangerous missiles, numbnuts," said Hazard, "or words to that effect."

"Now's our chance," said Drum. "Any smoke grenades?"

Brock unslung his Bergen and pulled out two grey canisters. "What's the plan?"

"We'll roll them into the other passageway," said Drum. "Hazard and the rest of the team will keep them busy while you and me make for the control room. The launcher will provide us with some cover and make them think twice about opening fire."

Hazard reached into his Bergen. "Throw this as well. It's a flash-bang. Should disorientate them for a few more seconds at least."

Charming hobbled over and stood stiffly with his back against the wall. Abdul joined him, clutching his arm. Drum looked down at Hamid and removed the boy's hands from his rifle. The AK swung heavily on its straps around the boy's small neck. Drum placed his hands over his own ears and nodded to Hamid to do the same. The boy quickly put his hands to his ears and screwed up his eyes. Drum gestured to Abdul. Abdul nodded and winced as he placed both hands over his ears. Blood streamed down his shirt and dripped from the elbow of his wounded arm.

Drum knelt and pulled the pins from both smoke canisters. He poked his head out and took aim at the other passageway, rolling each canister along the floor in quick succession. He had just enough time to see an insurgent raise his gun before crying out at the sight of the canisters rolling in his direction.

Mayhem broke out in the cavern as thick, grey smoke billowed from the two canisters, filling the insurgent's tunnel. Hazard calmly stepped out and lobbed the flash-bang, quickly plugging his ears with his fingers and retreating inside the tunnel.

A deafening bang echoed off the walls and roof space of the cavern. Hamid jumped and cried out and Abdul gasped.

Drum ran for the cover of the launch vehicle with Brock close behind him. Smoke was filling the cavern. Up in the control room, a technician frantically banged on the glass window trying to attract the attention of the guards. The other technician appeared to be working a radio. Drum guessed he was trying to recall the men from the village. He tapped Brock on the shoulder and pointed up at the man. Brock understood. He took aim and unleashed a burst of automatic fire. The control room window shattered, sending a rain of glass shards onto the floor below.

Covering fire issued from the team's passageway. Drum needed no more prompting. He dashed towards the base of the stairs and looked up just in time to dodge the falling body of a technician. It hit the floor with a sickening thud.

There were two levels to the stairwell. Drum raced up to the first level, leaping two steps at a time, the frame of the structure shuddering and clanking with each booted footfall. He turned to ascend the second stage when a shot rang out from above. The round clanged against a pillar and zinged past his head. Blood trickled down into his eye.

A burst of gunfire came up from below. The metal stairway sang out with the hits of rounds and their ricochets. There was a thud from above and a clanging sound as a pistol bounced down the stairs towards him. Technician number two, thought Drum.

Brock raced up the stairwell.

"You hit?"

Drum felt the side of his head and looked at his blood-covered fingers. He blinked and wiped away the blood streaming into his eye.

"Just a graze. Let's move."

More gunfire issued from the team's passageway, keeping the

insurgents busy. They responded hesitantly with return fire. The smoke had now drifted and obscured half of the cavern. Drum guessed the ventilation system would soon clear it. They had no time to lose.

They reached the last stage of the stairway, stepping over the body of the last technician. Drum entered the small control room, his boots crunching on the shattered glass. The place was a mess. He looked out of the destroyed window and down onto the floor of the cavern. He could just make out movement in the insurgent's tunnel. The smoke was clearing fast. Hamid looked up and gave him a hesitant wave.

"Found it?" asked Brock.

Drum drew back from the window and looked around the room. On the far wall was a large junction box. Several cable runs entered the box from below. On the front of the panel were two red handles, each labelled in Russian.

"This could be it," said Drum. "But my Russian isn't good enough to translate the signage."

"How hard can it be?" said Brock. "One of them must be 'Open' and the other must be 'Close'."

Drum leaned out of the window and tried to follow the cable runs coming up from below. He noticed a set of cables leading to the mobile launch vehicle.

"Or one handle could be 'fire one' and the other 'fire two'," added Drum.

Brock frowned. "I take your point. But they're mobile launchers. Why would they fire them from inside the facility?"

Drum nodded. He looked at his watch. "We have less than fifteen minutes to decide."

Brock stepped forward and grabbed one of the handles. "Fuck it. We're dead anyway if we stay here." He yanked the handle up.

23

The whine from powerful electric motors spinning up filled the cavern. The twin blast doors shuddered and moved apart, sending a vibration through the floor and walls. Brock let go of the handle which sprung back into its original position on the panel. The whine of the electric motors slowly faded and the doors ground to a halt, leaving a two-metre gap between them.

"You lucky bastard," said Drum, smiling.

"Who dares, opens the doors," added Brock.

A radio set squawked on the bench in front of them—a Russian voice urgently repeating the same request. Drum guessed it was the other team in the village. They would soon be en route back to the base when they received no reply. The radio operator had been successful in raising the alarm.

Drum looked down to the floor below and noticed movement around the enemy position. Men were trying to outflank the team in the passageway by using the launcher as cover.

"Enemy movement near the launcher," said Drum. "Try to pick them off. We need to move the team out of the tunnel and to the door."

Brock opened fire, aiming to pick off his targets with single shots. Drum waved to Hazard, beckoning him to move. Hazard nodded and squatted down on his haunches, firing single shots through the dissipating smoke at the enemy position.

"Charming, get moving, man," shouted Hazard.

Charming grunted and with an effort pushed himself off the wall. Abdul stood and placed his good arm around the soldier, his other arm now useless, his rifle dangling from his neck. The pair hobbled out into the exposed space behind the launcher. An insurgent shouted and rushed from the tunnel through the thinning smoke, firing off a burst of gunfire. Charming raised his rifle but was too late. A round took him in the shoulder, spinning him around and sending him and Abdul crashing to the floor.

Hamid cried out and ran towards the oncoming insurgent, his finger hard down on the trigger of his AK47. The weapon rattled off several rounds before the recoil knocked the boy backwards onto the floor. The insurgent thudded to the ground, unmoving. A stream of white smoke hissed loudly from the missile suspended above him.

Drum cried out to the boy.

"Run, Hamid!"

Hazard leapt from the cover of the passageway and grabbed Hamid roughly by the arm, pulling the boy to his feet.

"C'mon lad. Shift yourself."

Drum watched as Hazard dragged Hamid behind the shelter of the launcher. The insurgents, emboldened by the move of their comrade, crept from their position, firing short bursts of gunfire. Rounds struck the tail end of the launcher with loud clangs and pounded the floor around Charming and Abdul. Abdul cursed as a bullet took him in the leg.

"Cover me," shouted Drum.

"Wait, Ben!"

Drum ignored the warning and flew down the stairs, leaping over the last stage of the stairwell onto the concrete floor. He ran over to Charming and Abdul as a second insurgent rounded the tail-end of the launcher. Drum fired once at point-blank range into the man's face, felling him instantly.

Brock fired off several rounds from his vantage point in the control room, picking off two more insurgents trying to flank the team on the ground.

Drum grabbed Charming by the collar and dragged the big man beside Hamid. He went back for Abdul who was already crawling towards the launcher, his leg leaving a blood trail behind him.

"Time to go," said Drum. "The doors are open."

Charming laughed and spat bloody phlegm onto the floor. "I admire your optimism, Cap, but I'm done."

"Don't quit on me now, Corporal," said Drum, but his voice betrayed him.

Charming looked at his watch. "Ten minutes before this mountain comes down on top of us." He sighed. "I'll only slow you down."

"Corporal ..."

Charming gripped Drum by the arm and pulled him towards him. More rounds exploded around them as the insurgents moved towards their position. He pulled Drum close to his face. "You're the reason we're all here, Drum. If you don't make it, it's all been for nothing. Take the boy." He nodded at Abdul. "Me and him—we'll hold them off. You ain't got long."

Drum was about to argue when Charming roughly pushed him away.

"Now do your duty, Captain Drummond, and fuck off."

Hazard pulled Drum back. "Time to go, Captain."

He turned to Charming and handed him two fragmentation grenades. "I was saving these for a special occasion ..."

"Thanks, mate," whispered Charming. "Just give me a shout when you need 'em."

Hazard nodded.

Charming handed one grenade to Abdul. The man gave him a toothy grin.

Drum grabbed Hamid by the arm and moved around to the front of the launcher. Hazard moved up behind him. The door was only six metres away.

Brock stopped firing. "I'm out. It's now or never." He started his run down the steps.

Gunfire erupted from the enemy position, ricocheting off the metal stairwell and the front of the launcher. Brock jumped the last few steps, slinging his Bergen in front of him, close to the launcher. He dived and rolled to a halt at the base of a massive tyre.

Drum opened fire but only got off a few rounds before being forced back by a hail of bullets.

"We're pinned down," shouted Drum.

"Wait," said Hazard. "I have an idea."

He shouldered his rifle and aimed at the suspended missile.

"What are you doing!" exclaimed Drum.

"Don't worry, it won't explode—at least I don't think it will. It's fuelled by solid propellant."

Hazard fired off several shots, hitting the missile squarely in the body just above the engine. Thick white clouds of propellant plumed from the puncture wounds emitting a terrifying, high pitched squealing noise. The cavern started to quickly fill with acrid fumes. The insurgents stopped firing. Some ran back choking to the safety of the passageway.

"Now Charming. Fucking do it!"

A grenade landed with a clatter on the concrete floor close to the insurgent's position, followed quickly by a second. Drum heard cries of alarm as the grenades bounced, spun and rolled to a stop.

"Now, now!" cried Hazard. He hefted Brock roughly to his feet. "Fucking move it!"

Drum grabbed Hamid by the arm and they sprinted for the door.

24

Drum stumbled through the open doorway, dragging Hamid with him. He squinted in the plateau's bright sunlight. Brock and Hazard crashed into the back of him.

"Keep moving!" shouted Hazard. "Head for the comms array, it'll provide some shelter."

They ran towards the heavy mobile vehicle perched close to the edge of the plateau. They were halfway across when two colossal explosions thundered within the confines of the cavern, followed by a huge fireball that erupted between the partially open blast doors. Drum felt the heat on his back as the force from the blast slammed into him.

Drum hit the floor hard, opening up the wound above his eye. Blood trickled down his face and neck. He sat up, blinking. A fat, black mushroom cloud rose from between the blast doors and into the bright blue sky, tainting the air with an acrid, sulphurous smell. Sharp, tiny rocks rained down around them from the mountain above like miniature meteorites.

Hazard lay prone on the ground, face down, tangled in the webbing of his Bergen. Hamid sat up, blinking, and stared in awe at the rising cloud.

Drum rose unsteadily to his feet. He shook his head and moved to Hazard. The man looked dead. He knelt and pulled him over, sitting him up. He dug out a water bottle from Hazard's bag and placed it to his lips, letting the water trickle into his mouth. Hazard coughed and opened his eyes.

"Nice work," said Drum.

Hazard grimaced. "We've got to get off this mountain before she blows."

"Wait, wasn't that the big one?"

"Just the grenades igniting the missile propellant," explained Hazard. "The best is still to come—and it'll bring the rest of the mountain down on top of us."

"Fuck," said Drum. He staggered over to Brock who was now sitting up, dusting grit from his shaggy hair.

"We've got to move. That explosion was just a taster." He pulled Brock up onto his feet.

Brock looked around him. "Where's Charming?"

Drum shook his head.

"Abdul?"

"They didn't make it."

Brock bit his lip. Drum left him to his thoughts and shuffled over to Hamid. The boy sat with his head down, sobbing quietly. Drum had no words to console him. Charming and Abdul were gone. He lifted the boy's chin.

"C'mon, mate. Time to go."

Brock ran over and gripped Drum by the shoulder. "Vehicles heading our way. Must be the remains of the Russian unit."

Drum stood and peered into the haze of the desert air. A line of vehicles was snaking its way up the pass and would soon be at the plateau. He walked to the comms array and looked over the edge. The rock face went straight down, but here and there were small ledges like the goat path that had led them here.

"This is our way down," he shouted.

Brock peered down. "You're joking!"

Hazard joined them. "No choice. Break out the ropes and secure them to the legs of the array. We each have sixty metres, tops. If we don't reach one of those ledges by then …"

Drum walked off.

"Where are you going?" asked Brock.

"I need to get information from the array. My equipment is still on the ledge somewhere up there."

Drum moved to the back of the large square vehicle. Both rear doors were closed. He yanked down on one handle and pulled the door open. Sitting inside was a technician speaking feverishly into a radio mic.

They stared at each other in surprise. The technician was an enormous man, young and fit. He blinked twice, then suddenly stood and pulled out a large knife. Drum drew his pistol and fired. There was the sickening click of an empty chamber. He was out of ammunition.

The technician grinned and kicked back his chair. He jumped forward, slashing his blade in a wide arc aimed at Drum's face. Drum moved back quickly, but not before the blade had sliced painfully across his chest. A bright red stain bloomed through his shirt and blood dripped onto the floor.

The Russian came a step closer, drawing back the blade for a killing thrust to the chest. Drum held his ground and seeing the move stepped to one side at the last moment. He grabbed the man's wrist and yanked him forward, pulling him off balance while bringing the butt of his heavy Browning pistol down onto his head. The man dropped his knife, went limp and crumbled to the floor.

Drum steadied himself and took a deep breath. Sweat and blood were running down his face and the wound from his chest was now bleeding freely. He quickly surveyed the inside of the vehicle and located the array's monitoring area. According to GCHQ, the main processor and storage device were stowed in a small box beneath the main console. He knelt down and found the box and gave it a good tug. It wouldn't budge.

He heard his name called. Brock stood at the bottom of the steps, a panicked look on his face.

"What the fuck are you doing?"

"I've got to get the primary drive for the array, but it's fixed beneath this console," said Drum pointing to the box. "I can't budge it."

Brock stomped over and pushed Drum to one side.

"Let me try."

He kicked hard at the box. There was a sickening crunch as his booted foot ripped the box from it's housing. It fell to the floor with a loud clatter.

"I guess that's one way," said Drum, picking up the dented box.

He found the hard drive and yanked it from its circuit board. He hoped it was still functional.

A massive boom echoed around the plateau. A shudder ran through the length of the vehicle as the rock beneath it transmitted the force of the explosion. A symphony of clatters and clangs rang out from the metal roof as the mountain above them rained down rocks and pieces of shale. An enormous boulder slammed onto the rocky ground outside and rolled ominously towards them. It crunched against the tail-end of the vehicle, pushing it back towards the edge of the plateau. There was a screeching of metal as the stabilising legs of the truck twisted and scraped along the ground to gain purchase.

"Jump!" shouted Brock.

Drum stuffed the hard drive into his trouser pocket and leapt onto the rock-strewn ground. Brock followed close behind him. Dense black smoke streamed through the blast doors and spread out across the plateau. Dull secondary explosions and the sounds of grinding metal emanated from within the cavern of the base.

Drum picked himself up, shielding his head from the small rocks that were still falling all around him. He stopped and listened. He thought he could hear a vehicle. A larger rock struck him on the shoulder and brought him to his knees.

"The Russians are here," shouted Brock. "Get up!"

Drum staggered to his feet and followed Brock to the front of the array. He had tied three ropes to the stabilising legs of the truck, which was now perilously close to the edge of the plateau. Hazard squatted close to the edge of the precipice, still armed with his rifle, his waist and groin area looped with rope and bound to the main rope by a series of carabiners. Hamid sat close beside him, staring blankly into space.

Brock handed him a three metre length of rope and a carabiner.

"Make yourself a rappel seat—let's be quick about it."

Drum wrapped the rope around his waist and buttocks. He squatted, tightening the rope around his crotch before tying the rope off in a tight knot.

The entire process took him less than a minute.

Brock finished tying off his own make-shift harness. He pulled two figure-of-eight rings from his Bergen and handed one to Drum. Drum formed a loop in his main rope and threaded it through the larger ring. He pulled this loop over the smaller ring; friction between the rope and the rings would act to slow his descent. He attached the carabiner of his harness to the smaller ring. He tugged on the rope.

"I'm ready to go," he said.

"Ready," shouted Hazard.

"Hamid," shouted Drum. He gestured to the boy to join him.

Hamid sat on his haunches and stared back at him. He shook his head.

They heard a screeching of tyres. Drum could just make out the front of a jeep, obscured by the smoke streaming from the blast doors.

Brock grabbed the boy and swung him onto Drum's back. The boy cried out in alarm and clung to Drum's neck, nearly choking him.

"Go, go!" screamed Brock.

A burst of automatic fire strafed the edge of the plateau and peppered the side of the comms array. Hazard opened up on full automatic fire which then abruptly stopped.

"I'm out!" he shouted.

A massive explosion shook the mountain. A second fireball erupted from the blast doors and the whole plateau shuddered beneath them. There were screams near the jeep then a loud screeching of metal on metal as the force of the blast wrenched the blast doors from their housings.

Drum loosened his rope and jumped backwards over the edge.

25

Drum had no time to think as he placed one foot below the other in a shaky rappel down the rock face. Hamid clung on tightly like a limpet. Drum strained to breathe from the weight of the boy clinging to his neck and from the thick acrid smoke that was now swirling around them. Smaller explosions continued to erupt from above, sending showers of small rocks and shale down on top of them. Drum glimpsed Hazard as he slid past on his rope, bounding off the rock face with both feet. The smoke curled thickly about him, obscuring any sign of Brock

He heard a screeching noise from above—metal shearing from metal. The rope slackened and they dropped as the tension in the rope evaporated. Hamid cried out and gripped Drum's neck even tighter. There was a loud clang and the rope became taught again, bringing their fall to a jarring halt. Drum grunted as his harnessed tightened around him. He looked up and saw the end of comms array hanging over the edge directly above them. He heard screams as a man staggered towards the edge, his body consumed by flames. The man toppled forward and fell towards them like a fiery phoenix.

Drum braced and pushed himself off from the rock face, narrowly avoiding the burning corpse as it plummeted past to the depths below. He watched it hit the rock and then, to his surprise, crunch to a halt on a ledge before continuing down to the valley below. Drum pulled on his line, tightening the rope on his belay ring, slowing him to a complete stop. He looked for Brock but still couldn't see him. He turned to his left and saw Hazard several metres below him. He had also stopped and was looking down at the ledge. He waved to Drum and pointed at the rocky outcrop. Drum gave him a thumb's up.

The screeching started above them once more and the rope jerked down, causing him to bounce and spin on the end of the line. The comms array had slipped further over the edge. Drum could now see the whole of the front cab suspended in thin air above him.

He tried to shout, but all that came out of his throat was a hoarse whisper. He swallowed and tried again. "Brock!"

He heard coughing above him and to his right, then the dulcet tones of his sergeant. "I'm coming! Give me a minute." Brock's backside swung into view as he came to a halt beside him.

"To your left," croaked Drum. "About twenty metres below us."

Brock looked down. "Looks like Hazard's already made it."

The rope jerked again. Brock grunted as his harness tightened. Bits of rock broke from below the cab and rained down upon them. Hamid cried out as a rock struck him on the back. Drum thought he had lost the boy.

"We've got to get off this rope," shouted Brock.

Drum needed no more persuading. He pushed off from the rock face and loosened his grip on the line around his belay ring. They slipped down the rope a few metres before swinging back in. Drum pushed off with his legs once more, slipping down the rope a further few metres. With each rappel, he dropped closer to the ledge, but his arms and legs were tiring fast and the cut above his eye was bleeding again, blurring his vision. He had to rappel faster.

Drum pushed off hard and let the rope slip for as long as he dared. The rope screamed as they dropped a further ten metres. Hamid shouted in protest and gripped his legs tight around Drum's chest. Pain seared through his open wound, making him lose his timing for the next push. They slammed into the rock face and fell another few metres. Shards of rock crumbled under his boots and cascaded onto the ledge below.

Drum yanked hard on the rope to slow their descent. The belay ring locked. They bounced and spun on the last few metres of rope just above the ledge. The scream of twisting and shearing metal echoed above them. The line jerked down another metre. Drum looked up and could now see the floor of the main cabin of the comms array floating in mid-air. He wondered what was keeping it from falling over the edge. He then heard a series of loud twangs. The array's stabilising wires were snapping.

"Don't stop!" shouted Hazard.

Drum felt a tug on the rope and they swung closer to the rock face.

He looked down and could see Hazard pulling them towards the ledge.

"You're almost there. A metre to go. Drop and untie."

Drum let go of the rope and fell crashing onto the ledge, his legs buckling beneath him as he hit the rock floor. Hamid cried out as he rolled off his back towards the edge. Hazard grabbed the boy by the scruff of the neck and yanked him back.

Drum lay there, looking up at the smoke-filled sky, exhausted, blood trickling into his eye. He felt a boot in his backside.

"No time to rest, Captain," said Hazard. "Unhitch and help get Brock onto the ledge."

Drum grunted and sat up, wiping the blood away. He blinked and fumbled with his carabiner until he'd unlocked it. He unhitched it from the belay ring and shakily stood up.

He heard grunting and puffing above him as Brock swung into view. Hazard tried desperately to grab the end of his rope and pull him towards the ledge. Several loud twangs rang out as the remaining stabilising wires of the array snapped. Brock swore loudly as his line suddenly slackened and he dropped several metres below the level of the ledge. Then, with a great screeching of metal, the untethered communications vehicle slid slowly over the edge of the plateau.

Drum threw himself on the floor and leaned over the ledge, his arm reaching down just short of Brock's outstretched hand.

"Hold my legs!" shouted Drum.

He felt two strong arms bind his ankles, allowing him to shuffle his torso further over the side. Brock's hand brushed his, then gripped his wrist.

"Unhitch!" shouted Drum. "Now! Now!"

Brock drew his knife and cut the rope with one sweep of his blade. Drum heard his shoulder crack as his arm supported the full weight of the man. Bits of rock and gravel bit into the open wound on his chest causing it to bleed profusely. Blood dripped from his shirt and down his exposed arm towards his wrist.

Large rocks and pieces of shale cascaded down from above. Brock's line went slack, then disappeared down the rocky precipice towards the valley floor. A loud clang and crash echoed above them as the comms vehicle tumbled end-over-end off the edge towards them.

Brock heaved himself up on his extended arm and onto the ledge. Hamid rushed forward and grabbed his collar and helped pull him up. A hand gripped Drum's belt and he was unceremoniously dragged back from the edge. He glanced sideways and glimpsed a large black tyre passing close to his head.

"Move back!" shouted Hazard.

Drum rolled towards the back of the ledge. Brock scrambled on hands and knees before falling with his back against the rock face. They heard a loud roar and watched as the remains of the array tumbled past them in a tangle of wire and steel.

26

Drum lay on his back, his eyes closed, listening to the wind race around the exposed ledge. Exhaustion swept over him as the adrenalin rush of the descent subsided in his veins.

"I could do with a smoke," said Brock, wearily.

Drum pushed himself up on his elbows. "I'd settle for some water."

Hazard slid his Bergen towards him. Drum sat up painfully and pulled a half-full bottle of water from the pack. He took a few sips and handed the bottle around.

"All we have to do now is get down from this mountain," said Hazard. He looked up at the sky which had turned to an orange hue through the smoke. "We only have a few hours of daylight at most. We'll freeze up here when night falls."

Drum rubbed dried blood from his eye and looked around. They had landed on a narrow ledge, perhaps a few metres deep. It was just an outcrop of rock, formed within a wide fissure. The ledge disappeared into the rock face on either side after about ten metres, cutting off any route down.

"You look like shit," said Brock.

"Thanks."

Drum eased himself over to the back of the ledge and tried to make himself comfortable against the hard rock. Hamid shuffled over and rested his head against his chest. Drum flinched.

"Let me have a look at that," said Hazard. "I may have a dressing."

Drum unbuttoned his bloody shirt to reveal a twenty-centimetre gash from his left collarbone, down across his chest, to his sternum, still weeping blood.

"Ouch," said Brock.

Hamid winced at the sight of the wound.

"Got to get this stitched up," said Hazard, retrieving a small medical kit from his Bergen. "You'll have a lovely scar."

"Old war wounds," pondered Brock. "Always impresses the ladies."

"Right."

"All I can do for now is patch you up with a few dressings," said Hazard. "Should last until we get you down."

"If we get down," said Brock, peering over the ledge.

Drum sat patiently as Hazard cleaned the cut above his eye and applied a closure strip. He dusted his wound with antibiotic powder and applied and taped a series of small dressings to his chest.

"Good as new," said Hazard, smiling.

Drum nodded and tried to smile as he carefully replaced his blood-soaked shirt. He had a sudden thought. He patted the side of his trouser pocket, reached in and pulled out the small hard drive.

Brock rolled his eyes. "I hope that was fucking worth it."

Drum hoped so too. He turned the small device over in his hand. How many men had died getting him here for this? The crew of the Hercules; Charming; Abdul; and he didn't even know if Weekes and his team had faired any better. He stuffed the drive back into his pocket and zipped it up. He laid back and stretched out his legs.

Hamid sat up with a start and cocked his head to one side, listening.

"What's up?" said Brock.

Hamid stood and walked to the far end of the ledge. He listened intently, then gave a series of three quick whistles.

"Who's he whistling to?" said Hazard, standing.

Drum looked around, but all he saw were the jagged shapes of the rock face etched in shadow from the setting sun.

Brock stood. "I hear it. An animal bleating."

Hamid whistled again and the bleating grew louder. A small goat appeared just below the end of the ledge. It peered up at Hamid, bleating mournfully.

Drum pushed himself up and stared down at the goat. "There must be a ledge down there—hidden in the shadows."

Hamid jumped up and down and clapped his hands in joy, a broad smile across his face. He pointed to the goat.

"Well, at least we have something to eat," said Brock. "But how does that help us?"

"Where's there's a goat, there's a path," said Drum. "At least, that's what Hamid is probably thinking."

As if on cue, Hamid searched the rock where the ledge petered out. He leaned out and grabbed onto a handhold, pulling himself around onto the exposed cliff face. He searched and found a foothold below him, then another handhold, clinging to the rock with grim determination, a hairsbreadth away from a fall into the valley below.

"I can't watch," said Brock, covering his eyes with his hand.

Drum resisted the temptation to grab the boy; one false move on his part might cause him to fall. He bit his lip and watched his slow descent.

Hamid looked down then crabbed sideways across the rock face. The goat followed him, bleating loudly. He stretched down with his other foot but found no purchase. With one last effort, he reached out with his hand and grabbed hold of a rocky crevice. His small bony legs scrambled to find another foothold, but there were none. He hung there, clinging on by just his small, thin fingers.

Drum leaned out over the edge, trying to see where Hamid had got to. The fading light and deep shadow made it difficult to judge distance. The boy looked to be just above the goat.

"Drop," shouted Drum and gestured with his hand.

Hamid looked down and let go. He hit the ledge, falling hard onto his backside. He looked up and waved. He stood and looked around before taking a few steps along the path and disappearing around the curvature of the rock face.

"Did the skinny little runt make it?" asked Brock, peering through his fingers.

"He did," said Hazard, smiling.

"Blimey!"

Hamid reappeared a few minutes later. He spread his arms wide, showing the width of the ledge. He beckoned to them to come down.

"I hope he isn't thinking we can climb down there," said Brock, shielding his eyes to get a better view of the ledge.

"Stop your moaning, man," said Hazard, strapping on his Bergen.

"I'm just saying, I'm not good with heights."

"How did you ever pass selection," asked Drum.

"I kept my eyes closed."

"I'll go first," said Hazard. "Drum next, then our brave sergeant."

Hazard moved to the far end of the ledge and inspected the rock for handholds. He looked down and planned his route. He stepped onto a small outcrop of rock and pushed himself out and around onto the cliff face, grasping a crevice in the rock with his fingers. Without pausing, he stepped down and found purchase with his other foot. He pushed off and grasped a handhold below him. With his hand firmly gripping the rock, he swung the final half metre using just the strength of his arms. He landed with a crunch of his boots and looked around him, then un-shouldered his Bergen.

"Easy," he said. "There's plenty of room and it isn't far. Take your time, Drum."

Drum wondered if he had the strength for the climb. Hazard made it look easy—even carrying a Bergen.

He followed the same route. There seemed to be plenty of handholds and crevices and he felt relieved. He stepped onto the same rocky outcrop and pushed himself out. He reached and found his first handhold and gripped the rock with his fingers. His legs and arms felt like jelly. He looked around for his next foothold and found another rocky outcrop to his right. He stretched his leg down to reach for the rock with his foot. It seemed firm. He dropped his weight onto the rock and reached for his next handhold. Hazard was standing just below him, his arms outstretched. He felt the rock crumble beneath his foot. With one last effort, he pushed off and dropped, collapsing onto the floor of the ledge below. Hazard grabbed his arm and pulled him from the edge. Drum lay with his face in the dirt, breathing hard.

"That could have gone better," said Hazard.

Drum got to his knees. "Right."

Brock made a better job of the climb. Despite his initial protests, he kept his cool and both Hazard and Drum were soon easing him down onto the ledge.

"I hate climbing," said Brock. "This ledge had better lead somewhere."

The ledge was as wide as Hamid had shown them. They could easily traverse it, albeit in a single file. The boy was waiting for them at the first bend, an amused smile on his face. The sun was now setting fast, casting long shadows in their wake. They would need to move fast if they wanted to get down before dark. They rounded the bend and Drum was thankful to find a wide meandering path that led gently down.

"Right," said Hazard, adjusting his Bergen. "Let's get off this mountain."

27

Marchetti pulled up close to the intersection of Water Street and Fulton, a stone's throw from the South Street Seaport Fish Market and a few blocks away from the Petrov building. He killed the engine of his prized Corvette and sank back into its plush leather seat. The throaty chortle of the big V-8 engine continued for a few seconds more, before finally shuddering to a halt.

He loved this part of downtown Manhattan. He used to bring his wife from his second marriage here—or was it his first—he couldn't remember. The hazards of living a clandestine life. Lengthy trips abroad away from home did not make for a happy marriage. The car had been a present to himself after his second divorce. The 1969 Corvette Stingray was a Chevrolet classic—at least, that's what he'd told himself when he'd handed over a cheque for close to fifty thousand dollars.

It was six o'clock and the Friday commute was now in full swing. Bars were filling up and city workers were kicking off their shoes at the start of the weekend. As if on cue, he heard the staccato tap of heels approaching the car. He glanced in his side mirror and confirmed it was Seymour-Jones. He leaned over and opened the passenger door, careful not to hit the curb and damage the racing-green paintwork.

Harry bent down and poked her head into the car. "Sorry I'm late, Jack. Bloody Mandy wouldn't stop talking. Woman's a nightmare."

"No problem," said Marchetti. "I've not been waiting long."

He watched amused as she expertly shimmied herself into the passenger seat, despite her knee-length pencil skirt and bright red heels.

"Bloody hell, Jack. Why do you drive such a ridiculous car?"

"It's a classic."

"It's not very comfortable."

"I guess women weren't as tall in the sixties," said Marchetti, a little defensively.

"Sorry, Jack. It's just that my father bought something similar—an E-Type—shortly after he divorced my mother."

"You don't say."

"My mother said he was having a mid-life crisis."

"Really."

"I'm not saying you're having a crisis, Jack. But I mean … isn't it a bit flash for an undercover agent."

"Flash?"

"You know … conspicuous."

Marchetti smiled. She was right, of course, but he would not admit it.

"People see the car, Harry. Not the person driving it. And anyway, it's just another piece of American Muscle in Manhattan."

She returned his smile, but he could tell she saw through his bullshit. He changed the subject.

"Let's talk about the operation. I think we've taken it as far as we can. It's time to call it a day."

She shifted in the seat to face him. "But Jack, we're so close. Jimmy's sure he'll be able to identify the bank facilitating the money laundering, then we'll nail Petrov for sure and the bank."

"Delaney's man, Miller?"

"Yes," said Harry. "I just need a list of wire transfers and SWIFT codes of the facilitating bank. That should be enough to implicate them both. The DOJ then put the squeeze on the bank and they give up Petrov."

Marchetti had to admire her guts and determination. She had moxie, that was for sure. But he knew from bitter experience that such determination often got young agents killed.

"Sorry, Harry. It's too risky. I've spoken to Delaney. She agrees we have enough to go after Petrov for insurance fraud—possibly arson. No sense pushing our luck."

He watched as she turned away and slumped back into her seat, disappointed.

"Wrap it up, Harry. Make your excuses. You've done an outstanding job."

He tried to judge her take on the plan, but the gathering gloom made her expression unreadable. She turned to look out of the window. Her body language told him she was pissed.

"Hey, have you eaten? There's a great seafood place just off Fulton."

She turned and gave him a half-smile.

"Sorry, Jack. I promised Jimmy I'd have dinner with him tonight."

Marchetti turned and reached for the keys in the ignition, feeling a little deflated. "Hey, no problem. I'll give you a lift uptown. Put your seatbelt on."

The V-8 engine roared into life, its power pulsating up through the seats and throughout the length of the car, before settling into a throaty beat.

"Oh, wow!" exclaimed Harry.

Marchetti allowed himself a smile of satisfaction. "Its why it's called American Muscle."

He floored the accelerator.

28

Harry spent much of the next day watching Mandy eat her way through a packet of Oreos; the woman seemed to have an endless supply of the cookies hidden inside her desk drawer. It was close to six o'clock and Harry was growing impatient for her to leave for the evening. The door to their small office opened and the ever cheery Jonathan poked his head in.

"Hey, guys. I'm heading for the local watering hole. Anyone want to join me?"

Mandy crammed the rest of her cookie in her mouth and pushed back her chair. She waved her arm and grabbed her coat from the rack.

"How about you, Harry?"

Harry gave an exaggerated sigh. "Sorry, Jonathan. I need to finish this report for upstairs."

Jonathan gave her his best lopsided smile. "OK. See you tomorrow. Don't work too hard."

Mandy grinned as she swallowed the cookie. It wasn't a good look. "Yeah, hun. Don't work too hard."

Harry waited for the elevator to chime, then gave it a few more minutes before moving to Mandy's desk. There were cookie crumbs everywhere. She opened the drawer and found it crammed with packets of Oreos. She carefully removed them to reveal Mandy's crib sheet of passwords taped to the bottom. She found the item she was looking for, marked 'EFT Room' followed by a four-digit code. Electronic Funds Transfers were how most major corporations moved money around the world electronically. Harry knew that Mandy used the room at least twice a day. Why she couldn't remember the code was beyond her. Brain the size of a pea. Only room for Oreos and men.

She repeated the code to herself, then replaced the contents of the drawer.

She felt a pang of guilt. She had sworn to Marchetti that she would end the contract today. *Illness in the family, Jonathan. I need to be in London. Apologies to Mr Petrov.* At least, that was the plan. She knew Marchetti would be pissed if he found out she was still here.

But they were so close. All Jimmy needed were the bank codes used for transferring dirty money, and the case against Petrov and his London bank would be airtight. She had to do it.

She logged off her terminal and grabbed her coat and bag. The EFT room was one floor down. She left the office and headed for the stairwell. She didn't want to risk bumping into anyone at the elevator.

The door to the stairwell gave a loud click as she pulled it open. She looked around, but this part of the building was now empty. She started down, her heels tapping on the bare concrete steps. She stopped and removed her shoes, padding in bare feet the rest of the way and exiting onto the next level.

The floor looked identical to the one above. Where her office should have been was a room with a solid-looking door and a keypad. She looked around and waited. The offices on either side appeared empty. *They've all gone home,* she said to herself. She took a deep breath. *It's now or never.*

She replaced her shoes and walked over to the door. This had to be it. It was the only secured room on the floor. She punched Mandy's code on the keypad and the door clicked opened.

Well, that was easy peasy.

Overhead lights flickered on as she walked through the door. There was little in the room except for a long computer desk in the centre and a row of filing cabinets along the back wall. On the desk sat three workstations, all powered on. She closed the door and took a seat behind the desk.

The screens of each workstation were black and lifeless. A small, green LED flickered at their base. *They're still processing,* she thought. Cables from each workstation fed into a central box beneath the desk. She was no computer expert but she knew enough to recognise the box as a network hub. The room was on its own private network—detached and inaccessible from the general network of the main building. This was common with systems that dealt with sizeable amounts of money. It was one reason Mandy had to visit the room to execute a transfer. But while their physical security was good, they had a vulnerability.

And Mandy O'Donnell, you are the weakest link!

Harry guessed the screens were in power-save mode. She tapped the space key on one terminal and the black screen brightened. A logon screen popped up. She stared at the screen for a few seconds. Be a dear, Mandy. Don't let me down.

She typed in Mandy's user-id and password—she was betting they were the same across all systems—and pressed ENTER.

The logon screen blinked off and a series of menus appeared. She heaved a sigh of relief and marvelled at how someone as incompetent as Mandy was ever let loose on such a sensitive system. She examined the menu options.

All EFT systems looked different, but essentially they all did the same thing. If you had the right authorisation and knew the banking codes and accounts of each counter-party, you could transfer millions of dollars over the ether with the press of a button. And modern systems recorded every detail of the transfer, logging the route through every facilitating bank.

Harry knew that to transfer funds internationally required a wire transfer. This was an electronic bank-to-bank transfer using a private network called SWIFT. The Fed kept a close eye on it.

Harry found the menu option for 'wire file upload'. She needed a copy of this file. It contained all the bank codes and accounts needed for each 'wire'. She pressed the option and the screen displayed a submenu: Upload; Print; Edit. She had it!

There was no printer in the room, but she pressed 'Print' anyway. She knew most systems had an option to print to a file. The print menu popped up, and she entered a filename on the local drive. She removed a pen drive from her bag and looked for a USB port on the desktop workstation. There didn't appear to be one. So close, yet so far. Out of curiosity, she clicked on the file, which opened in a spreadsheet. She was shocked. There were hundreds of wire transfer instructions, some for millions of dollars. This should have been a red flag for any reputable bank—especially a London bank. She had to get this file to Jimmy. Then she remembered the email system. But was it enabled on this network?

Harry heard the elevator chime outside.

Shit!

She searched the desktop icons and found the email application. She clicked on the icon and Mandy's email account opened. She hurriedly composed a new message, addressing it to Jimmy Miller. She clicked 'attach' and the file menu appeared. But where did she save the file?

She heard footsteps outside the door and the beeping of the keypad. She dragged her eyes back to the file menu. Where are you? Of course, on the desktop. She attached the file and pressed SEND, then logged off. The computer screen dimmed as it returned to power-save mode.

The door opened and a burly guard stepped in. He glanced in her direction, then stepped to one side to allow an irate Mandy into the room.

"Get away from there!"

Harry pushed back her chair and stood up.

"Take it easy, Mandy. No need to get yourself worked up."

Jonathan walked into the room followed by two serious looking guys in dark suits. These must be the corporate muscle, thought Harry.

Jonathan stood and stared at her, shaking his head. "This is very disappointing, Harry. I was looking forward to working with you."

Mandy stepped closer and pointed a painted nail in her direction. "I told you this skinny bitch was too good to be true."

"This is all a misunderstanding, Jonathan," said Harry, giving him the best smile she could muster. "I was looking for the ladies' room. Must have got myself lost."

"I don't think so, Harry," said Jonathan, pointing up at the ceiling. "Caught on camera, you see. Triggered an alarm when you entered the stairwell. This is a restricted area—for good reason."

Harry looked up at the ceiling. God, how did she miss that? Marchetti had been right. She'd overplayed her hand.

Jonathan nodded in her direction. The two suits moved to her side and held her securely by the arms.

"Mandy, be a dear and check the terminal," said Jonathan.

Mandy stomped over to the desk and hit the spacebar on the keyboard. The screen came to life. She logged on and brought up the EFT application and rapidly went through several screens of information.

"I can't see any obvious changes to the system," said Mandy, peering at the monitor. She turned around, her face flush with anger. "What did you do, bitch!"

Harry prayed she wouldn't see the extraneous file on the application desktop and tried to bluff it out.

"Nothing, Mandy. I couldn't log on."

"Liar!" shouted Mandy, and punched her hard in the stomach.

Harry doubled over, winded.

"Now, now, ladies. Let's not get into this now. We'll get the tech guys to go over the system in the morning." He checked his watch. "We need to get her uptown. Mr Petrov would like a word."

They dragged Harry from the room and into a waiting elevator. Harry felt queasy from the punch in the stomach and the smell of Mandy's cheap perfume within the enclosed space. They exited to the lobby.

Harry scoured the lobby for anyone she knew, but the area was empty. No one stayed late in the Petrov offices. The two suits held her securely, one on each arm, as they marched her out of the building and bundled her into the back of a black Range Rover. She felt like a slice of salami as they squeezed in beside her. The thought made her feel nauseous once more and she needed to breathe. Jonathan dismissed the driver and got behind the wheel; Mandy clambered into the passenger seat beside him. She twisted around to face Harry.

"Comfortable, hun?" she smirked.

Harry thought she might retch.

"Open the window, will you? I think I'm going to be sick."

"I'll do it," said Jonathan, pressing a button on the centre console. "Don't want you throwing up."

The roadside window wound down, letting in a light breeze. Harry leaned towards it and took a deep breath. Headlights flashed once from across the street. She stared at the sleek lines of a Corvette and her heart lifted as its engine roared into life.

29

Marchetti had watched as the two thugs bundled Harry into the back of the SUV. *Shit, Harry. What have you done?*

He had flashed his headlights once, hoping she would notice, wedged as she was between Petrov's two goons. He recognised the guys: hitmen, courtesy of the local Russian mafia. They'd be armed to the teeth. It would be difficult to extract her without a major gun battle. Two of Petrov's minions were in the front of the vehicle. They wouldn't be a problem. He turned the key in the ignition and the Corvette's engine burst into life.

The SUV took off, heading for South Street. *They're using the FDR, which means they're probably heading for Petrov's apartment on the Upper East Side,* he reasoned. He activated his phone.

"Operations, Charlie, India, Alpha."

The call was instantly connected to the CIA operations centre in Manhattan. The voice that answered was calm and efficient.

"Operations," said the voice. "Challenge word of the day is 'Britannia'".

Well, that was apt, thought Marchetti. He gave his ID.

"Foxtrot, Charlie, Tango, Zero, Zero, Nine."

He pulled out into traffic and followed the SUV from a few vehicles back.

"Randel here, Mr Marchetti. What do you need?"

"Tactical. One unit. Marksman."

"Timeframe?"

"The next thirty to forty minutes. First Avenue Tunnel, heading North."

There was a pause on the line.

"I've assigned you Marcus Hemings."

Marchetti had heard of Hemings. An ex-Seal and a crack marksman.

"Good, give him my number. I'm in pursuit of a black Range Rover. Get him to call me."

He ended the connection and concentrated on keeping up with the SUV. The FDR was heavy with traffic and he'd fallen farther behind. There were now four vehicles in front of him. He put the pedal to the metal and the V-8 roared like a wild beast. He overtook a slow-moving Prius and cut up a brand new BMW. Make way for American Muscle. The Beamer gave an angry blast of its horn.

His phone rang. "Marchetti."

A softly spoken man with a Texas drawl replied. "Hemings."

"Where are you, Hemings?"

"Just leaving Greenwich Village. What's your ETA?"

Greenwich Village, thought Marchetti. He's on the West side of the Island. It would be tight. He glanced out of the window. It was the end of summer and the sun was waning over the East River. He glimpsed the Brooklyn Navy Yard.

"Lower East Side. Approaching the Williamsburg Bridge. Traffic moderate to heavy. I estimate …"

"About forty to fifty minutes then," interjected Hemings. "I should make it. What's the target?"

"Black Range Rover," replied Marchetti. He gave Hemings the plate number. "Five occupants. Two heavies in the back chaperoning a tall red-head. They'll be heavily armed. I need the woman alive."

"An extraction," said Hemings. "What about the two in the front?"

"Expendable."

"What's the plan?" asked Hemings.

I've no idea, thought Marchetti.

Harry heard the roar of the Corvette behind them and a car horn sound, either from anger or impatience. She fought the temptation to look around and kept her eyes fixed on the road ahead. Marchetti wasn't exactly being inconspicuous.

"Whoa," said Jonathan. "Some guy in a Corvette behind us cut up a Beamer."

One suit turned around.

"He tails us."

Jonathan stared back at him in the rearview mirror and frowned.

"Just some jerk in a muscle car, that's all."

"I don't think so," said the suit on Harry's left. He reached for the water cooler behind his seat and came back up with a small submachine gun.

Harry flinched at the sight of the weapon.

The suit passed the gun across Harry to his colleague and went back for another weapon.

"Jesus, guys," said Mandy. "I think you're overreacting."

"Drive faster," replied the suit.

Jonathan pulled out sharply into a gap in the traffic and accelerated up close to the vehicle ahead. They heard the Corvette behind them.

"He's coming up fast," said Jonathan, furtively glancing into his mirror. "I'm boxed in."

The suit behind Jonathan looked around.

"Slow down."

"What? You just told me to speed up."

"Slow down. I take him." He pressed his window button and the black-tinted pane of glass rolled down with a soft purr. He shifted around in his seat and extended his gun out of the open window, back towards the Corvette, now one car back.

"No!" shouted Harry and lunged, shoving him hard against the door.

The submachine gun kicked upwards, harmlessly firing off a burst of rounds over the tops of the vehicles.

The suit cursed and elbowed Harry hard in the face.

Marchetti heard the sound of gunfire before he saw the submachine gun pointing in his direction. He braked hard and swerved into another lane. Cars immediately behind him did the same, swerving and braking, setting off a cacophony of screeching tyres and angry horns that spread like a wave down the FDR. A black sedan in front of him wasn't so agile. It braked hard and spun out of control, smashing into the concrete barrier separating the northbound and southbound highways.

Marchetti pulled back, putting distance between him and the SUV. This was escalating fast.

"Hemings. Still there?"

"I'm coming up to the Flatiron building on Fifth. Where are you?"

"Coming under small arms fire."

He glanced to his left, across the southbound highway. He glimpsed the Chrysler building emerging from between the high-risers, its silvery cladding painted with an orange glow from the setting sun. "Just passing the East Village."

"Good," said Hemings. "You need to get them off the FDR and onto First Avenue. Force them off at Exit 9 - that's East 42nd Street. Then they'll have to head for Second Avenue and back via East 40th Street. That will bring them back to First Avenue. If they're heading to the upper Eastside as you suspect, they'll keep on First and pass under the tunnel close to the UN building."

"Agreed," said Marchetti.

They needed a choke point and the First Avenue tunnel was their best shot. There was also less risk of collateral damage. It all depended on Hemings getting to the tunnel before he did.

"Will you make it?" asked Marchetti as an afterthought.

"I'll make it," replied Hemmings. "But you must stop them just before the tunnel entrance, otherwise I'll have no line of sight."

"Understood," said Marchetti.

They were coming up to Exit 8 and the Midtown Tunnel. He needed to act fast. Exit 9 was just a few minutes away. He hit the gas and the Corvette leapt forward, its engine growling like a wild thing. The SUV was somewhere up ahead. He had to force it onto the exit ramp.

The FDR started to rise, a gradual curving elevation in the highway, like a giant roller-coaster. The green sign on the gantry overhead told him that Exit 9 was just a half a mile away. Keep right, keep right. He swerved into the outside lane, almost colliding with a Yellow Cab, and accelerated past to a blast of angry horns. The SUV came into view, speeding in the middle lane.

Up ahead, the tall, oblong brick of the United Nations building rose beside the East River and, coming up fast, the off-ramp to Exit 9 on his right. He stomped down on the accelerator and the engine screamed in protest. He'd never red-lined the engine before and he hoped the aged V-8 didn't explode. He pulled up alongside the SUV and glimpsed the driver through the passenger-side window. He pressed a button on his console and the window wound down. The smoky, polluted air of the Manhattan Parkway rushed in. With one hand on the wheel and one eye on the road, he pulled his gun—a Desert Eagle, chambered with a forty-four Magnum. It was a ridiculously big gun with a round large enough to take down an elephant—or in this case an SUV. He stooped over the wheel and pointed the gun up at the driver. It had the desired effect.

The SUV swerved into the right-side lane, heading for the exit ramp. Keep right, keep right. Marchetti braked, dropping the gun onto the passenger seat, and cut across two lanes of the Parkway. A large articulated truck flashed its lights and swerved to avoid the Corvette, barely missing the rear of the car. Marchetti let out his breath as the wailing sound of its horn faded into the distance.

The exit ramp was coming up fast and Marchetti knew he would not make it. He braked hard and spun the wheel. The Corvette's tyres screamed in protest and the back of the car started to fish-tail. He spun the wheel in the opposite direction and the Stingray slid against the yellow barrier dividing the two lanes with a sickening crunch.

Marchetti winced at the sound of scraping metal. He fought with the wheel, bringing the Corvette back onto the exit ramp. He floored the accelerator and gave chase to the SUV.

Marchetti watched as the Range Rover headed for 42nd Street. He hung back. This was not a good place for a shootout.

"Where are you, Marchetti?" said Hemings.

Marchetti could hear vehicle noise over the phone and the occasional curse as Hemings navigated the Manhattan traffic.

"Coming up to 42nd Street. Target is half a click ahead of me. Where are you?"

Marchetti heard a long, drawn-out curse which could have been 'shit' but which sounded like 'she-et'.

"I'm running behind schedule. Heading South on 2nd Avenue, just passing 44th Street. Had to take a detour to beat the traffic."

"They're just ahead of you," said Marchetti, "but you're not going to make it."

"Suggestions."

It was all in the timing, thought Marchetti. The situation was fluid. He had only one suggestion.

"Improvise."

Harry held her face and tried to stem the flow of blood dripping from her battered nose. She froze as the cold steel of a handgun pressed against her temple.

"I kill her now," said the suit on her right.

"Not here," said Jonathan. "We need her alive. That's what Mr Petrov ordered."

Harry heaved a sigh of relief as the gun was removed. She heard the angry growl of the Corvette coming up fast on her left.

"Doesn't this guy ever give up?" said Jonathan, nervously checking his rearview mirror.

Harry caught sight of the Corvette as it slid alongside. The window rolled down.

"Fuck, fuck, fuck!" shouted Jonathan, and swerved into the nearside lane. The big SUV rolled dangerously over to its left and then to its right before levelling off and speeding up once more.

"Where are you going!" shouted Mandy. "You've taken us off the Parkway."

"The guy pointed a fucking cannon at me. He was going to blow my head off."

"He forced you off the highway," said the suit on Harry's left. He racked back on his submachine gun and lowered his window.

"Put the guns away," said Jonathan into his rearview mirror. "We're coming up to the UN building. There will be cops and security personnel all along this stretch of the highway. We can't afford to be pulled over." He paused. "Anyway, I think we lost him."

Jonathan slowed as the exit ramp rose above the FDR and banked around to their left. Harry watched as the UN building slid by on their right.

"Where are we?" said Jonathan.

"We're coming up to 42nd Street," said Mandy. "We need First Avenue. That will take us straight up to the sixties and from there Madison Avenue."

"It's one way," said Jonathan in frustration. "How do I get back onto First?"

Harry jerked forward as the car braked and stopped at the lights. She looked around, still clutching her swollen, bloody nose. She recognised the lights of Midtown. If Marchetti was planning something, he'd better do it fast. The sun was setting and they were losing the light.

"Keep on until you hit 2nd Avenue," said Mandy. "Then hang a left and go around the block. That'll take you down 40th Street and back onto First."

"Gotcha."

The car moved off, giving way to the occasional late crossing pedestrian. Harry noticed several police vehicles lining the street. Jonathan was right: there were police everywhere. But she was invisible behind the black-tinted windows. Mandy nervously scanned the street, now crowded with people heading for the theatre district.

The two suits sat back, relaxed but attentive, their submachine guns resting in plain sight on their laps. Just another day in the hood.

The SUV purred down 2nd Avenue. There was no sight nor sound of the Corvette. Jonathan relaxed a little as they rounded the corner and headed up East 40th Street. They passed more police vehicles parked up against the sidewalk. Road signs ahead told them they were approaching the intersection to First Avenue and the United Nations building. They rolled to a stop at the lights.

"Looks like we lost your friend, Harry," said Jonathan, glancing back at her in his mirror. "Sorry about the nose."

"Yeah, sorry hun," said Mandy, smirking as she looked out onto the bustling sidewalk.

"Fuck off," replied Harry.

An old Ford pickup pulled alongside them, its paintwork weathered to a rusty patina. Harry was drawn to the sound of the engine's throaty chortle, a sharp contrast to the soft purr of the Range Rover. A good ole boy in a battered Stetson lounged behind the wheel. The lights changed the pickup pulled ahead, leaving them in a cloud of exhaust fumes.

"That can't be street legal," mused Jonathan, as he pulled the SUV into a wide arc through the intersection.

The United Nations building loomed up on the right as they completed their turn. Signs overhead warned them to keep left. Up ahead, the twin black maws of the tunnel descended beneath the First Avenue blacktop.

There was a screeching of tyres behind them. Harry turned and saw the Corvette expertly drift around the intersection, its front tyres at an acute angle, fighting for grip. A patchwork of bright yellow scrapes now decorated one side of the car's racing-green paintwork. The V-8 roared as it completed its turn and accelerated toward them, its rear tyres burning rubber in a cloud of white smoke.

"Jesus!" cried Mandy, "watch out."

Up ahead the rusty Ford pickup had stopped side on to the tunnel entrance. Jonathan cursed and braked hard, bringing the Range Rover to a grinding halt in the middle of the road.

Harry fell forward and ended up facedown between the two front seats. She pushed herself up in time to see the guy in the cowboy hat peering down the sight of a long rifle from behind his truck. She ducked her head back down. There was a loud crack and the windscreen shattered. A body fell heavily across her back, pinning her to the floor of the SUV. All she heard next was Mandy screaming hysterically.

She peeked to her right and watched as the remaining suit scrambled out of the passenger door. He stood in the middle of the road, facing back the way they had come, and fired off a sustained burst of rounds. He paused to eject the spent magazine. Too slow. Harry heard a loud boom and the man spun around, falling in a heap on the ground. He lay there, sprawled on the blacktop, a hole the size of baseball punched through his chest.

"Harry?"

Harry heaved herself free from the body pinning her to the floor and pushed herself up. Jonathan's headless remains lay slumped across the wheel. A pale-faced Mandy sat shaking in the seat beside him.

"Jack?"

She clambered out unsteadily onto the road. The stocky figure of Marchetti stood in silhouette against the dying light of a Manhattan sunset, an enormous smoking gun in his hand.

Not Goodbye

30

"I'm sorry about the car, Jack."

Marchetti glanced behind him at the wreck of his prized Corvette, now double-parked outside the British Airways terminal at JFK. A bright, yellow scrape marred the once pristine paintwork, and both door panels now featured an array of impressive-looking bullet holes.

He sighed. "Nothing a bit of Bondo and a lick of paint won't fix."

"Really!"

"Nah. It's fucked."

Harry gave him a quizzical look. She stepped forward and kissed him tenderly on the cheek.

"Thanks, Jack."

He hated goodbyes. He'd spent his entire career avoiding them. But he had to admit he would miss Harry. He checked his watch.

"Well, I don't want you to miss your flight."

She smiled. "It was nice of the Agency to buy me a business class ticket."

"Yeah, well, you earned it."

"Really, Jack? I feel I screwed up. I should have listened to you …"

"Hey, hey. What did I tell you?"

"No regrets."

"Right. No regrets. You made a call."

"And people got killed."

"Shit happens—especially in this business. And those guys were scumbags. They would have killed you."

"You saved me, Jack. I won't forget that."

"Yeah, well …"

She glanced over his shoulder at the Corvette. "And thank God for

American Muscle."

"Yeah, that helped."

Harry snapped the handle up on her cabin bag. "Hey, who was the cowboy?"

"Navy Seal. Sharpshooter. He took a risk firing through the windscreen. Hell of a shot. Took out the driver and the thug in the back with one round."

Harry looked down at her feet.

"What will happen to Mandy?"

Marchetti gave her a wry smile. "She's singing like a bird. Negotiated some deal with the DA. She's giving up the entire Petrov network."

"That's good …"

"Couldn't have done it without you, Harry."

"Thanks, Jack."

"So …" said Marchetti, looking at his watch.

"Time to go. London will be boring after this."

"Boring's good, Harry. Make the most of it." Somehow Marchetti didn't think she would.

"Goodbye, Jack."

Harry grabbed her bag and walked off towards the terminal entrance.

Marchetti watched as she disappeared into the crowd. He knew that Delaney had made her a generous offer to come work for her in New York. His gut told him he hadn't seen the last of Seymour-Jones. No, not goodbye, Harry.

He turned and looked at the wreck of his car and sighed.

31

They buried Prakash in the mountains. It felt the right thing to do. He had been born and raised in Nepal in the sight of a mountain, and it seemed fitting that he now rested in the shadow of another. He had no family to speak of in his native homeland and, in his adopted home of England, his only son had requested the burial. Brock had been uncomfortable with this at first until Drum reminded him that there were no mountains in Sevenoaks.

Saying goodbye to Charming was more difficult. His body lay entombed under tons of rock beneath the plateau along with Abdul. The mountain still smouldered like a funeral pyre two days after the attack, shrouding the village in a thick pall of haze. The people of the militia turned out to say goodbye to the two men. They stood in the courtyard of the shattered mosque and whispered their prayers. Aisha stood with the women and wept for her father.

On the evening of the second day after the attack, at the request of Asadi, the troop gathered in the militia's main compound for one last conference with the village elders. The women supplied them with food and drink and, much to the surprise of the Afghan men, Brock cooked a goat curry. He admitted he felt bad for the goat and assured Drum that it wasn't the one that had saved them in the mountain. Drum reckoned that it was the best thing he had ever tasted.

That evening, they asked Drum to recount his escape from the mountain. Aisha sat in the middle of the floor and translated, pouring tea for the men who huddled close to listen. He told the men of Abdul's great sacrifice and that of his new friend, Charming. Aisha wept softly at the retelling of her father's death, and the room fell silent until she had recovered her composure.

Drum continued with the story, praising the bravery and resourcefulness of the young Hamid and told Asadi that without the boy's help they would have all perished.

Asadi beamed at Drum's words and hugged and kissed his son. But Hamid did not smile. He looked sad and full of regret. Drum knew that look. He had seen it before on soldiers returning from combat when they sat with friends and family back in the safety of their homes with a blankness in their eyes, but he had never seen it in one so young.

Hamid had learnt the truth of war.

"Your words were well received, Captain," said Weekes. "You should have been a diplomat."

Drum wasn't sure if Weekes was being sarcastic, but nodded anyway.

Hazard entered the room and made his way over to the troop. He knelt beside Weekes and spoke close to his ear.

"Comms from HQ. They want us gone by first light. They've given us coordinates for an extraction. Black Hawk from Bagram airbase. The Yanks are keen to get hold of Drum's data."

"Looks like we're travelling First Class," said Poacher. "Have we time for more of Brock's curry?"

"That'll be your third," said Brock, pleased with the success of his cooking.

"Can't beat a nice piece of goat."

Drum wondered over the urgency of their extraction. The data could wait. The destruction of the mountain base had all but eliminated the threat to NATO forces in the area and the local militia was now hunting down those few insurgents that had escaped the conflict. When the Russian contingent had retreated to their mountain base, the attack on the village had collapsed, giving Asadi an outright victory. The local militia would return to their rightful homes once more.

"I suggest we wrap it up here for tonight," ordered Weekes. "Let's bid our hosts goodnight. We have an early start tomorrow."

Weekes told Aisha to convey their plans to Asadi and to thank him for his help. They all stood and Asadi formally shook each man's hand as they left the building. As Drum was about to leave, Asadi enveloped him in a firm embrace and kissed him on his forehead.

"Thank you," he said in English.

Drum gripped the man's arm and nodded. Hamid stood close to his father, his head down. Drum knelt and lifted the boy's chin until he was looking into his eyes.

"Thank you."

The boy threw his small arms around Drum and hugged him. Tears rolled down his cheeks. He buried his face in Drum's neck, trying not to show the rest of the men his display of emotion. But the fighting men of the militia knew how he felt and no one made a sound. They had all experienced the feeling, as all fighting men do.

Drum stood and looked down upon the young boy. He wondered if he would ever see him again. On a whim, he mussed up the boy's hair. Hamid looked up and smiled and a sigh of relief went through the men and they all laughed. A chant started within the throng, and second by second the chant beat louder.

"Drum, Drum, Drum ..."

32

Marchetti stood in Phyllis Delaney's spacious corner office and admired the view of midtown Manhattan. Delaney had done well for herself.

Officially, he was here to brief her on the Petrov operation and to learn more about the new organisation she had set up: Roderick, Olivier and Delaney. Langley was curious. Unofficially, he wanted to know what Harry was up to. He felt he owed it to the young Brit to steer her clear of any more clandestine operations that might put her at risk.

The door opened and Delaney marched in. "Mr Marchetti. Nice to see you again." She extended her hand.

"Call me Jack." He took her small hand in his.

Delaney was dressed casually for the fall in a pale, pink cashmere sweater and a dark tweed skirt that fell just below the knee. A pair of short brown boots completed the ensemble. Her only jewellery was a string of elegant pearls. Part of the monied set that entertained in the Hamptons at the weekend, thought Marchetti.

"Has anyone offered you coffee?"

"I'm fine."

Delaney gestured to a black leather couch by the window. "Take a seat." She took a similar-looking couch against the opposite wall. They assessed each other across an ornate Persian rug.

"I'm here to update you on the Petrov situation," said Marchetti. "Looks like he fled the country."

"That was careless of us," said Delaney, straight-faced.

"Yes, not the best outcome. We were a little slow locking down his private jet. Seems he anticipated our move."

Delaney looked down at her hands and examined her manicured nails. "I see."

Marchetti pressed on. "The good news, his entire operation is toast. He won't be funding any more terrorist activities—at least from the US."

"Where is he now?"

"Our intel says he's in London."

"London? So we can extradite him?"

"Eventually. British Intelligence has him on their radar. A person of interest. They'll want to have a word or two before they hand him over."

"I see."

"Talking of Brits, I understand you've offered Harry a job."

Delaney smiled. "Yes, she'll do well in the new organisation."

"Which does what exactly?"

"You can think of us as the Pinkertons of the Financial Services industry. We'll investigate financial crime and assist government agencies, should they wish it." She tilted her head to one side and gave him a puzzled look. "Why? Are you interested in joining us?"

Until she mentioned it, Marchetti had never considered working in the private sector. The thought took him by surprise. He composed himself and smiled.

"Langley's curious. I'll pass it on."

"Think about it, Jack. It's never too late to change course. We could use a person of your experience." She smiled. It was very endearing.

"Thank you for the offer, but deep down I'm just an old government guy. I'll leave it to the younger folk."

"The offer's on the table if you change your mind," said Delaney, standing. Marchetti guessed the meeting was over. They shook hands.

"She'll be back next month," said Delaney as she opened the door.

"Who?"

"Harry. I'm sure she'll want to meet you again, talk about the operation over a coffee. She'll need a mentor, Jack."

"Right."

"And I'm sorry about the car. She said you were very attached to it."

"She said I was having a midlife crisis."

"The Brits can be brutally frank sometimes."

"Right."

"She said she was saved by American Muscle."

"It's just a Corvette."

"I think she was referring to you, Jack."
Marchetti smiled. "Right."

33

"How did your meeting go with Rogers this morning, Alicia?"

Alicia Harwood, formerly of the British Trade Delegation in Moscow, stirred her coffee absentmindedly as she watched the people of Leadenhall Market bustle about with their day-to-day business. All, that is, except the flower seller opposite. He was one of theirs. An MI6 spotter. And the fishmonger next door. He was one of theirs. She looked up past the freshly painted colonnade that supported the glass roof of the Victorian market and caught the flash of a telescopic lens in the window above the pub on the corner. A marksman. He was also one of theirs. SAS, probably.

"Are you still with me, Alicia?"

She put down her spoon and smiled. "Sorry, Giles. I was thinking."

"So, how did it go?"

She frowned as she recalled the meeting in the offices of the head of MI6. It didn't go well.

"Oh, you know. The usual nonsense. Should have got down on my knees ... thought of England. The usual bollocks."

"Sorry, Alicia. I went to bat for you—"

"I know, Giles. The guy walks around like he's got a poker up his arse. Has he ever been in the field?"

"Apparently."

"Anyway, I'm on the exit ramp. Years of service down the toilet because I wouldn't suck the dick of some Russian bureaucrat."

Giles frowned. "What will they do with you?"

"Giving me to Treasury. I'll be working with Sir Rupert Mayhew."

"Our bagman."

"The very same."

Alicia scanned the market once more for their man. "Why meet us here do you think?"

"Petrov?"

"Yes. I mean, in the City. Could have met us anywhere. A hotel would have been better."

"As I recall, your last encounter with a Russian in a hotel didn't end well."

"Point taken."

"He's a Lloyds Name."

"Petrov?"

"Apparently so," said Giles. "Made money, and lost money. Nature of the beast when you're underwriting large risks. He owns a syndicate."

"Really, I didn't know."

"He's probably tying up loose ends before he hands himself in."

"What will we do with him," asked Alicia.

"The usual. We'll turn him and send him back. We have enough dirt to put him away for life."

"Not if his friends find out."

"Hence the precautions."

"Do the Americans know?"

"I think Rogers is playing this one close to his chest."

"Naughty."

Giles nodded. "Talk of the devil."

A man in a grey pin-stripe suit walked towards them. He casually looked around as he neared their table.

"Good morning," he said. "You must be my handlers."

Giles indicated a seat beside him. "Good morning, Mr Petrov." No one bothered to shake hands.

A waitress appeared from inside the small cafe and stood at their table. Alicia cast a discrete eye over her. Force of habit, really. You could tell a lot about a person from their attire.

"Espresso," said Petrov.

"Make that three," added Giles.

The waitress nodded and walked off, her heels tapping a staccato on the cobbled street. An expensive shoe for a waitress, thought Alicia. And what waitress wears heels to work?

"Have the arrangements been made?" asked Petrov, looking around him once more.

Giles leaned back on the cafe's rickety chair and smiled. "Of course.

And you're safe here."

Petrov grimaced.

"You've been in contact with your associates back in Moscow?" asked Alicia.

Petrov regarded her. He was trying to decide her importance in the scheme of things. Being a Russian man in his sixties, he concluded that Giles was the more senior officer and so paid her scant attention or deference.

"I have. I assured them that the London end of the operation is still intact. New York was just a setback."

"But you don't think they bought it," pressed Alicia.

Petrov turned to Giles, seeking permission to continue speaking with his underling. Giles said nothing and waited for Petrov to continue.

"They are naturally cautious. They want to see how things play out here in London. The destruction of the base in Helmand was a blow, but not a complete loss. We gained much from the operational test of the technology."

Giles nodded. "I see. How did you manage such a large construction in the area without being detected? It couldn't have been easy."

Before Petrov could answer, the waitress appeared with their coffees. She served Petrov first. A young thing, thought Alicia. Her shoes were probably a recent trend. She looked down at her own shoes. Simple plain courts with a low heel. A sensible shoe, as Giles would say. The waitress served the remaining coffees and retreated to the cafe. Tap, tap, tap.

Petrov unwrapped the amaretti served with the espresso, and took a bite. He crunched down on the hard biscuit and took a sip of his coffee. He sat back. The small espresso cup looked comically out of place in his large hand.

"It wasn't," continued Petrov. "We paid off many officials—Pakistan, Iran—but we couldn't have done it without the help of the local militia. A man called Asadi."

Giles had read the briefings from Helmand. This was at odds with the mission reports.

"And this Asadi assisted you with the construction?"

"At first. He supplied the local workforce and kept routes open to the Pakistan border. But he objected to some of our—how you say—methods. He became a problem."

"And the buyers?" continued Giles.

Petrov nodded. He took another sip of his espresso.

"We had several buyers interested in the technology." He paused, a confused look on his face. "We still have. Unfortunately, all the data we accumulated on the tests was lost or destroyed in the attack."

No, we have the data, you moron, thought Alicia. She noticed that Petrov was drooling. She reached across the table and stayed Gile's hand. "Don't drink the coffee."

Petrov stared across the table, blankly. His arm went limp and dropped to his side, the espresso cup falling with a clatter to the floor.

Giles looked down at his own cup. "Good Lord."

Alicia stood and placed a hand on Petrov's neck. "He's dead."

34

"Your man came through then?"

The afternoon sunshine of an Indian summer streamed through the windows of the Mayfair club and splashed its rays around the rim of McKay's glass of whiskey. The Glaswegian stared into the amber liquid, his mind back in the mountains of Helmand Province and the soldiers that now lay there, never to return.

McKay turned away from the library window and stood with his back to the empty fireplace. He and Rayner were alone. A private meeting. It was his second time in the club in as many weeks. If he turned up again, they'd think he was a member. He smiled at the thought.

Geoffrey Rayner tapped his glass, making a loud clinking sound. "I said your man did well, Major."

"Sorry, sir," said McKay, taking a large gulp of whiskey. "Long flight."

Rayner nodded. "I understand. You lost two good men. But you pulled it off. The mission was a success. Take comfort in that. Where's your man now?"

"Flying out of Bagram as we speak."

"And the data?"

"With GCHQ. They're having a field day. A mine of information, they say. The Americans are happy too."

"Good. Job well done. You should be pleased."

"I am, sir."

"But?"

"That last order ..."

"What about it?"

136

"The men weren't happy."

Rayner rose from the sanctuary of his armchair and stood to face McKay.

"Is this the reason you're here?"

"Yes, sir. The drone strikes on the militia's encampment did not go down well."

"I see."

"They … I don't understand the rationale for the attack."

Rayner turned and took a few paces to stand in the centre of the room, clutching his whiskey. McKay found the man difficult to read.

"Well, officially, the men don't need to understand the rationale for the attack," said Rayner. "And the army isn't in the business of making their soldiers happy." He paused and stared into the bottom of his glass. "But as the man who put this operation together, I suppose you deserve an explanation."

"Thank you, sir."

Rayner returned to his chair. "There was another operation in play. One that you weren't aware of."

"I see."

"An agent of ours. Well, technically not an agent—although I think Rogers of MI6 would like to make her one. More of an operative. Young English woman, working with the Americans. She helped bring in the Russian bagman."

"Bagman?"

"Yes, the Russian paymaster funding the operation. According to our intel, he made payments to this militia."

McKay was dumbfounded. "Asadi?"

"It looks like he was playing a double game. Taking money from the Russians while recruiting large numbers of followers to his cause. It made our American friends uneasy. A potential threat to the region."

"Or a potential ally," added McKay.

"Maybe. But that was a judgment call that had too made."

"I see."

Rayner stared unblinking at McKay. "Have you seen reports of the attack?"

"I have," said McKay. "The militia's compound was totally destroyed."

"And Asadi?"

"We have no positive confirmation, but we have every reason to believe that he was in the compound."

Rayner took a sip of his whiskey. "Job done."

"Aye."

"Time to get back to Helmand, Major."

McKay downed the rest of his whiskey. The meeting was over. "Sir." He moved towards the library doors.

"Will you talk to the men?"

"No, sir."

"No?"

"No sir. Drummond has resigned his commission and the rest of the troop are leaving the service. Their time is up and they are not re-enlisting."

"I see. And what about you, Major?"

"I resigned my commission before leaving Helmand. I won't be returning to Afghanistan."

"I see." Rayner stood and extended his hand. "Then I thank you for your service. If there is anything I can do, let me know."

McKay looked down at the hand and considered not taking it. He couldn't afford to make powerful enemies. He shook it firmly. "Thank you, sir."

McKay walked out of the club and into the warm sunshine. His first day as a civilian. He wondered what he would do now? He wondered what Drummond would do? Their last meeting had not gone well. The men blamed him for the drone attack. There would be no happy reunion with Drummond and the rest of the troop.

Be the first to hear about discounts, bonus material and much more! Subscribe now and never miss an update.

My readers are important to me, which is why I like to keep them updated with the latest news and release dates for new novels and other bonus material that I'm working on. I do this by sending out the occasional newsletter which contain special offers and new bonus material.

If you are <u>not</u> already subscribed, simply use the link tomasblack.com/omega-news

P.S. You can unsubscribe at any time.

Tomas Black was born in the UK. After graduating from the University of Sussex, he taught for several years before taking a post graduate Diploma in Computer Sciences. He spent the next twenty five years working in the City and other major financial centres around the world as a computer consultant, specialising in the Audit and Security of financial systems. He now travels and writes.

Printed in Great Britain
by Amazon